Fiction Favours the Facts

by Mark Morgan

Bible
Tales
www.BibleTales.online

ISBN (eBook): 978-1-925587-21-0
ISBN (Paperback) 978-1-925587-20-3

Cover pictures by Philip Morgan.

Free Download

Paul in Snippets

An 81-page PDF novelette by Mark Morgan.

The life of Paul painted from the Acts of the Apostles.

Get your free copy of *Paul in Snippets* when you sign up for the Bible Tales mailing list. As well as the eBook, you will receive a weekly email newsletter with micro tales, informative articles and special offers.

Visit **http://www.BibleTales.online/free-pins**

To my ever-patient wife Ruth.

Introduction

This book contains a collection of micro-tales that were first published in every second issue of the weekly Bible Tales newsletter between 28 July 2016 and 10 August 2017.

You may ask: Micro-tales? What are they?

Quite simply, they are short stories about Bible characters or events. Some are about Bible characters you may never have heard of, while others concentrate on an incident in the life of one of the more famous Bible characters.

BibleTales Online produces Bible-based fiction – the facts of the Bible rounded out with imaginative detail to help readers participate in the lives and feelings of real people.

I hope you enjoy this collection.

Mark Morgan
www.BibleTales.online
August 2017

Contents

Part Two - New Testament   **105**

Acknowledgements and thanks

Particular thanks go to Ruth, my wife, who helped me find time to write, patiently read what I wrote, and humoured me when I spent inordinate amounts of time on research into minute details.

Cathy, my oldest daughter, has tirelessly undertaken the thankless task of copy editing and proof reading each of the stories before they were published in the newsletter, and has also reviewed the entire manuscript. Thanks, Cathy.

Thanks to Philip, my youngest son, who drew the two pictures of herons used on the cover.

Feedback from a few newsletter subscribers has also improved the stories, so I thank them.

Almost all of the pictures come from the vast collection of illustrated Bible stories hosted by FreeBibleimages.org. The original illustrations used are copyright Sweet Publishing, and the digitally adjusted compilations from which they are taken are copyright FreeBibleimages. No alterations have been made.

The images are made available under a Creative Commons Attribution-ShareAlike 3.0 Unported license. (https://creativecommons.org/licenses/by-sa/3.0/).

Four public domain pictures are used in the stories: three from openclipart (www.openclipart.org) and one from Wikimedia Commons. These are acknowledged where they are used. All pictures have been reduced to greyscale for printing.

A request

In all of my books, I have a request to make of all readers: if you find any errors; typos, spelling errors, poor grammar, unkempt use of vocabulary, or, most importantly, errors of fact where the story misrepresents the Bible, please let me know. I can't correct printed books, but electronic versions and any new printed editions can be fixed.

Part One: Old Testament

One

Cain's Confessions

For the true story see Genesis 4:1-16; 1 John 3:12.

Where do I start? A few things went wrong in my life and I'm the one who has to suffer for it all. Much of the time, it really wasn't even my fault.

Abel was a good enough brother when we were young, but as we got to be adults he started becoming a know-it-all and such a goody-goody.

I shouldn't have killed him, I know that, but I wouldn't have done so if he hadn't been so sickeningly "righteous".

The whole family knows the story now, but my side of it rarely gets any fair consideration. It makes my wife quite angry at times.

Of course, "the whole family" means all of the world, and I'm the one they all look down on because they wouldn't have done anything like that. Sanctimonious, self-righteous and smug – and everyone tells me I need to control my temper. It makes my blood boil when I hear it.

I was the older brother, and took up growing plants and vegetables quite young. Since I didn't really want competition, I was quite pleased when Abel showed an interest in looking after sheep instead.

Things seemed to be going well until Abel wanted to show just how holy he was. God likes us to acknowledge that we are sinners, so we go through the motions and offer sacrifices. Well, I am a horticulturalist, so I gave an offering from the delightful produce in my garden. Sumptuous potatoes, perfect pumpkins, carefree carrots and luscious leeks. Shocks of tall waving wheat and some gargantuan grapes. Carefully culled from the furrows I struggle to keep free of weeds – weeds that grow so wonderfully since Mum and Dad made such a mess of this world. If only they had followed instructions we would all have been better off. It makes gardening really hard work, not to mention all the bugs and things that like to feed on my crops too. We just have to get used to the fact that sometimes when we bite on an apple we get a bit more than we bargained for!

But never mind that, I brought these offerings and you might expect that God would be pleased with them. A gardener bringing a gardener's offering. A tiller of the soil bringing the produce of the soil. Makes sense? Well of course it does.

Abel followed my example and did the same, bringing some of his spare sheep and presenting bits of them to God.

Cain and Abel bring their offerings[1]

Well, God accepted Abel's offering and rejected mine. All those beautiful turnips and tasselled corn cobs were just worthless in God's eyes. Only the pathetic remnants of some cute little lambs would satisfy God, and I just don't grow those things. Animals are such noisy and dirty things, and they cause so much trouble everywhere. Give me a nice calm line of radishes over a messy bunch of bleating lambs any day.

And what irked me even more was when God asked me why I was angry! Surely it's obvious that I'm going to be angry when my little brother is praised for giving something that he had easily available, while my offering is cast back in my face? It shouldn't be any surprise, and it's not my fault either.

God told me that if I did well I would be accepted, suggesting that I knew that what I had done was wrong, and that I had to rule over sin instead of giving in to it, but

---

[1] Sweet Publishing/FreeBibleimages.org:
http://freebibleimages.org/illustrations/003-cain-abel/ Slide 3

he wouldn't explain to me what was wrong. No comment at all, nothing to help me learn, just blame, blame, blame.

Now I ask you, what was God getting upset about? All that he would tell me was that I had not "done well". Now, I ask you, what does that mean? He wouldn't tell me, and as we talked I got angrier and angrier.

As soon as we finished talking, I went looking for Abel and suggested that we should go out into the field. He probably thought I wanted his advice about what offering I should make. Maybe he planned to give me instructions about what grapes I should give to God, or maybe he hoped to sell me one of his flea-bitten sheep, but either way I didn't give him the chance.

He's dead now, and although I suppose I shouldn't have killed him, he really got what he deserved. I did my best to control myself, but he just seemed to have such a smug expression on his face that day. He knew that I always get angry easily, so what did he expect? If he'd had any brains he wouldn't have come out with me into the fields. But he came, and that put the cat among the pigeons.

Naturally, my anger and feeling of being badly treated went with me. Naturally, I wanted to take it out on him. Naturally, I can't do anything to make a dead man alive again.

When Abel was dead, I was really sorry, but I couldn't help feeling that he had brought it on himself. Fortunately, I had a spade with me, so I buried the body and went back home.

Everyone wondered where Abel was. I'm sure they wouldn't have cared half so much if it had been me missing. Even my wife was asking where he was. I suppose he was her brother also, but her questions made me angry too.

Then God talked to me and asked me where Abel was. He dismissed my evasive answer and told me that I was going to be punished with a special punishment aimed just at me.

God cursed the ground specifically for me, so that even using all my skill as a gardener wouldn't make things grow well for me. No longer would I be able to settle down and be a happy and contented farmer. Instead, I would have to wander around finding food as best I could. The punishment was overwhelming. I knew that if God said it, he meant it, and despite the way God had treated me, I still didn't want to be sent away from him either.

To be honest, I was also concerned that if I had to keep wandering around, I would not be able to build a strong, safe house that could keep out any eager vigilantes who decided to try to make me pay for killing Abel.

God listened to my complaints and gave me a solution. Ever since, though, it has seemed to me that his solution might have been worse than the problem. God put a mark on me so that everyone could recognise me. It didn't matter much at the start, since there weren't very many of us, but nowadays there are a lot more people around and whenever anyone meets me, they either know who I am already, or they ask me what the mark is from. No-one else has a mark like mine, and I have been very glad to see that it hasn't passed on to our children.

God said that he was putting the mark on me so that no-one would kill me – and I'm still alive, so I suppose it has worked – but more than that, it has made me think every day about what I did. Every day makes me consider my actions of long ago, and it isn't making me any more sorry for what I did. Abel has ruined my life. First he showed me up before God, and now he shows me up before anyone who meets me. I even find my wife looking at that mark when I'm sounding angry.

Despite the fact that we have to keep moving, I am determined to build a family of my own and to worship how we want to worship. My wife supports me completely in this now, and we're sure to outnumber the do-gooders soon, so we will be able to defend ourselves if they ever attack us to try to punish me.

Overall, I'm a bit sad that Abel isn't here anymore, but there's no doubt whose fault it was – and it wasn't mine! It seems to me that even God agrees; after all, Abel is dead and God has put a special mark on me to protect me from being killed. He didn't protect Abel in that way!

I'll keep worshipping God my way, thank you very much, and I think everything will work out alright. After all, doing things "God's way" didn't help Abel, did it?

Two

A Blissful Silence

For the true story, see Genesis 6 and 7.

Forty days: all day, every day; rain, rain, rain. Finally, this morning, the rain stopped.

Just yesterday, we sensed a difference in the incessant flow of rain that had been so utterly consistent. Instead of the steady, heavy drumming of rain on the roof of the ark – never easing for a moment – there were times when, for a few minutes, the volume of the ceaseless noise actually reduced. During those times, visibility out of the window was noticeably better too.

But very early this morning, I woke up. With the slight disorientation of sudden wakefulness, it took me a while to work out what had woken me, but I finally understood: it was the silence and stillness outside.

Down inside the ark, it is not easy to tell what the time is, or even whether it is light outside or not, so I climbed to the window platform and looked outside. The window was very cleverly designed to make sure that no rain could get in from any angle, whatever the intensity of the rain or wind. It worked wonderfully, but the platform was a very noisy place to be during that first forty days. After a while it made your ears hurt, and there wasn't anything different to see anyway.

On this morning, however, things were different. It was still very early and the coming of a new day showed only in the faintest hint of a glow in the east. The sky was clear and the stars were brilliant in the moonless sky. A great stillness seemed to be spread over the face of the water, and the reflected stars moved gently in the calmness. Smooth and still, the earth seemed almost to be resting after a titanic struggle, and an overwhelming feeling of peace filled me.

No longer would God look on the earth and see evil and violence, and, for the first time, I began to wonder what would happen to the new earth. Savouring the present silence, but dreaming of a new world in which we could live without fear, I stood and watched the light slowly grow in the east until, suddenly and silently, a golden path was drawn across the waters between me and the flaming disc which slid effortlessly above the uninterrupted horizon. Water, and only water surrounded me in every direction. No visible birds or fish, boats or islands, mountains or coastlines. We were entirely alone.

But being alone on the face of the waters did not mean we were alone in the ark. Maybe the animals had sensed a change, or maybe this was simply their normal dawn chorus without the competing noise of the rain, but whatever the reason, the noise within was a cacophony and it was clear that the animals needed their morning attention. I couldn't keep ignoring them.

I took a last look around the watery vista with its unexpected beauty. Ever so gently, a breeze was beginning to play on the waters. Since then it has strengthened until the unending sound of wind[2] has replaced the drumming of rain in our ears. But that was still in the future as, turning, I left the window and went about my work.

Everyone was euphorically happy that morning. Even the animals seemed to be glad that the time of unrelenting destruction was over. After forty days, we had all become accustomed to the idea that our acquaintances, our neighbours and even our relatives were all dead. We knew that there would be no exceptions and that somewhere down there in the newly-still water was the old life we had left behind. Many people we would not miss. Violence had been a way of life for them and a freedom from the fear of their brutality was something we had all enjoyed as the ark rose up on the waters. Others, however, had been good friends who we would miss, friends on whom we had expended much effort in warning them about the coming flood. But none had believed us enough to come with us. None could see that the Creator's coming judgement was just. And we couldn't keep them as friends and obey the Creator. When push comes to shove, you have to make choices. We made ours. Sadly, though, they made theirs too, and so we went into the ark by ourselves. Just our family, alone.

---

[2] Genesis 8:1

The last year had been the worst – a very trying time for each of us. It was only when we had been in the ark for two or three days that I realised how much stress we had been under. Those harrowing times must have made us finish the work faster, but I know that there were times when my father wondered whether we would all make it into the ark alive. I don't know why people get pleasure out of making others suffer, or why they like to intimidate and harass at every turn. My wife must surely have been looked after by an angel when that group of young women decided to attack her at the well, first verbally and then physically. No-one recognised the man who came to her aid, and I certainly couldn't find him later to give him my heartfelt thanks. If I could have found him, I would have invited him into the ark too. But I guess his work had been done, and we were all so thankful.

I won't go through the list of other near misses and terrifying incidents which convinced us to keep putting the finishing touches on the ark even through the hours of darkness in those last few weeks. We only slept when we just couldn't keep our eyes open anymore. And we didn't go to any of the community meeting places either if we could possibly avoid it, and never alone. After the incident with my wife, my father, my brothers and I took our largest containers and filled them from the well in the middle of the day. Our women didn't go there again. But that took precious time and left the ark unprotected too. We couldn't afford to do that either after the "accident" six months before when we had returned unexpectedly early to find our neighbour gently fanning the flames of a small grass fire towards the ark. He had assured us that he had been fighting the fire, which had started by accident, but it certainly hadn't looked that way.

"Love your neighbour" was the lesson our father and mother had taught us. Our father had told us that if we wished to walk with God, we needed to be like him in this way, so we really tried. But it was certainly a case of unrequited love. Our neighbours hated us and most of them had taken specific actions to make us suffer. Complaints about everything we did. Stolen materials and equipment. Ropes that broke unexpectedly. The list seemed endless, but now, I just want to forget about it all. What hurt us most was that even the people who loved us and would never have tried to hurt us personally, even they would not make any stand at all to help us.

Animals went into the ark by the thousand[3]

Then, on the tenth day of the second month, seven days before the rain started, God's final instructions had come to my father.[4] In that last week we were far too busy

---

[3] Sweet Publishing/FreeBibleimages.org:
http://freebibleimages.org/illustrations/009-noah-ark/ Slide 9
[4] Genesis 7:1-4

to worry about anything but doing exactly what he told us. Each day, thousands of animals had to be taken inside and put into the safest places possible. They were all utterly docile, but even so, we were incredibly busy. All the food had to be double-checked and properly organised. No-one came near us to cause trouble during that whole week, and it was almost as if God had put a fence around us. Late on the sixteenth, we finished with the animals and everything was ready.

During the night, we dismantled the boarding structures and stowed them aboard – we would need them for unloading the animals at the end. Ham went round with the pot of liquid pitch and daubed all the places where they had been attached while Japheth made a final round of the supports around the ship to make sure the ark could float freely away from them. My father and I went over the entire roof and window structure, knowing that these would be severely tested the next day. It was a difficult and dangerous task in the dark, but my mother and my wife belayed the ropes and neither of us slipped badly.

Towards dawn, we finished these last-minute tasks and got ready to go aboard for the last time. Collecting the last few things that we needed from our home, we climbed up into the ark just as the light of day began to diffuse abroad under the leaden sky. We were exhausted and went straight down into our living areas, intending to sit down for a while before coming back to have a last look around to make sure we hadn't forgotten anything. However, as we reached our living quarters, we heard a gentle thud from above. Not a loud noise, but it sounded final, somehow. I rushed up to the door and found that the chocks we used to hold the door open had all been removed and sat in a pile in the corner. The door was shut. It was a big door, but I could normally move it a bit by myself. I pushed as hard as I could, but the door didn't move. God had shut us in.[5]

Only a few moments later, the rain started. Heavy, pounding rain. Rain that made the roof resound like a drum, with us inside the drum. The noise of the rain continued to grow louder over the next few minutes, but that was all we heard from outside. Of the people, our neighbours, we heard nothing. Within minutes the ark was floating, and for the next few hours we had a rather rough ride.

I tend to be the one who likes to work with numbers as a bit of a game, so after we had been sailing for thirty days, I tried to work out how much manure we had moved from the various animals. It took a while to compute, but when I got the answer, it made me glad that my father had started us on the job straight away. A couple of days of leaving that to build up would have made the job overwhelming.

Well, that's all I have time to write at the moment. Animals are hard task-masters! Although it will be much easier to dump the manure over the side when it isn't raining, I'm sure it will always keep us busy for any part of the day when we're not feeding them. Fortunately, it is never unmanageable – each day's work can always be completed as long as we start early and work hard. It keeps us fit and we always go to bed tired. No spare time to muse, and maybe that is for the best. Perhaps when we land I'll have more time to write.

---

[5] Genesis 7:16

Three

An Afternoon at the Well

For the true story, see Genesis 24.

Tomorrow, I should see my future husband for the first time.

The servant tells me that we should arrive at their camp in the late afternoon, as long as we start early in the morning and don't get delayed.

I'm feeling rather nervous about it, although I'm glad that God has chosen my husband for me.

To be honest, it's good to leave home, too. My brother Laban can be a bit overbearing. He runs the house and coerces my mother into doing what he wants. I really didn't want him choosing my husband! I was also getting the impression that one of his friends was interested in me, and I don't like any of Laban's friends.

Since my father Bethuel had a stroke a while ago,[6] Laban has taken over more and more, and I admit that I don't like it, so it's good to be out of there.

My "escape" came about in a way that Laban couldn't really prevent – and anyway, he was rather pleased with the valuable gifts that were given.

I want to write down how it all happened so that I don't forget what took place and how God intervened to make sure that I could marry my cousin Isaac. Well, actually, he's not exactly my cousin because we come from different generations – our family tree is a bit mixed up that way. It's really my father Bethuel who is Isaac's cousin, but soon he will be his father-in-law, so that will make it feel as if we are in the same generation anyway.

So, let's start at the beginning with a bit of important background. In our family, I have the job of collecting the water from the well. That normally means going early in the morning to collect what we will need during the day, and again in the early evening for the water we need for the night. When we have visitors or other special needs, there are sometimes extra visits at other times as well.

Water is heavy, and making sure that we have enough available keeps me busy, as well as rather thankful that I am naturally quite strong.

That particular evening, I took the water jug to the well a little earlier than usual, and it was clear even before I got there that something was different from normal. It looked as though a small trading caravan had come to

---

[6] There is no evidence that Bethuel had had a stroke, but there are hints that he was not the one who made decisions in the family or even that he spoke much. See Genesis 24:28, 29, 53 and 55.

visit. A man was sitting a short way from the well, looking tired and hot, with a few servants and some camels nearby. Now these sorts of men can be a bit of a handful at times, and I was the first to arrive at the well, although several other women were in sight. Groups of men travelling around, far away from their womenfolk and their homes, sometimes have a tendency to make life difficult for young women like myself. I hoped that these men would be too tired to cause trouble.

Rebecca with her water jar[7]

As I approached, they seemed to notice me, but they didn't move or say anything – which at least alleviated my initial concerns. They looked harmless enough from closer up. In fact, the man who was obviously the leader of the party had a rather pleasant, friendly face. He smiled slightly in my direction but remained seated.

I walked down to the spring and calmly filled my jar with water, being quite eager to fill it and leave as quickly as I could – just in case.

---

[7] Sweet Publishing/FreeBibleimages.org:
http://freebibleimages.org/illustrations/isaac-wife/ Slide 9

Then, just as I lifted the jar to my shoulder and started to walk away from the spring, the leader of the men surprised me by jumping up and running towards me.

My heart was in my mouth as he stopped in front of me and said, "Please give me a little water to drink from your jar." He was carrying a cup and held it out towards me.

He smiled again, and I quickly swung down the jar from my shoulder and rested it on my hand.

"Have you come far?" I asked, as I poured the water into his cup.

He took the cup and put it to his lips eagerly. It was clear he was thirsty.

"Not too far today," he answered after taking a long draught and wiping his lips with the back of his hand, "but our longer journey has been from Canaan. It has been a long way, and some of the people we've met haven't been very friendly."

"I'm sorry to hear that," I said, and offered him some more water. "Drink, my lord," I urged him, filling his cup again. Once more, he drank eagerly.

After a few swallows, he took the cup from his mouth and said, "Ah, that is good! It's been a dry day for us." He emptied the cup and added, "Thank you. That will be enough for me."

The other men were all watching us, and they looked rather thirsty too. Even the camels were gazing at my burden with interest. They had seen the small amount of water that had spilled when I had taken the jar off my shoulder, and were stirring.

"I will draw water for your camels also, until they have finished drinking," I said, well aware of the magnitude of the task I was committing myself to.

I knew it would be hard work, but a visitor is a visitor and these men need to be treated as visitors should be treated. They deserved better treatment than they had been receiving so far in my country.

Near the well there was a trough for watering animals, so I quickly emptied what was left in my jar into the trough and went back to the well. Fill the jar; empty it into the trough. Fill the jar again; empty it into the trough. By then the leader had brought his camel to the trough and the beast was eagerly drinking the water. Before I came back with the fourth jar, the trough was almost empty and the other camels were being led towards it as well.

The leading man stepped back and watched. He didn't offer to help, and I was glad because that is not how we do things in Nahor. I was the hostess and it was my job to look after them. My family has always insisted on showing hospitality, and I love it. I wasn't doing anything special that day to get attention or anything: it's just what our family is like.

By then some of the other women from the town had arrived for water too. I'm sure they would have helped me if I had asked them to, but I knew that they would all be in a hurry to return to their families, so I just greeted them and kept working.

Ten more jars full and the first camel seemed satisfied. The other camels were still waiting for their turn, and I suspect that at this point the leading man was expecting me to give up when the first camel finished. He watched me in a questioning, wondering, excited way as if something important was happening.

"Let the other camels have a drink too," I urged, a little short of breath, but determined.

"Alright," he replied, somewhat doubtfully, but still with that excited look. "The other men can get their own water, though – you don't need to do that."

I suppose I was grateful for the small reduction – although it would only save me one jar full – but I knew there would still be many, many jars of water to be brought to the trough.

When camels are thirsty, they drink a lot, and it took me more than an hour to satisfy them. Even then, I'm not sure that they were completely satisfied. Towards the end, the men were discouraging the camels from drinking much, and even dragging them away from the trough. I heard a rumour that they brought the camels back to the trough again later in the evening, and some of the servants spent another hour or so topping them up!

Nevertheless, for the time being, the camels had finished drinking. That was when the leader went to his camel and came back with a beautiful solid gold nose ring and two heavy bracelets, also of solid gold. I was utterly amazed.

He asked me whose daughter I was and when I answered, he told me that he was a servant of my father's uncle Abraham. Can you imagine how I felt? You see, Abraham is well-known in our family for his hospitality and generosity. In fact, I have tried to model my attitudes on what I have heard of him, and now that has brought me to marry his son – though I didn't know that until later.

We invited the men to stay at our house for the night – we always have lots of spare food for any visitors and their animals – and while they were there, the leader explained what had happened. He described how he had been sent by Abraham to find a wife for Isaac, and how he had set up a test to let God show him who was the right wife for Isaac. And straight away I had come along and done everything that he had asked for! No wonder he'd had that waiting, watching, excited look. Every little detail he had specified, I had done. And yet I had done it of my own free will. He hadn't suggested it, nor had there been any angel whispering in my ear telling me, "Rebecca, go and water those camels." What an amazing God we worship! How did he organise that?

If I hadn't been generous with the water for the camels and someone else had been, none of this would have happened for me. Abraham is a rich man, so his only "real" son is a very special catch as a husband. That's probably the only reason why Laban was happy with the arrangement, but that's not how I felt, or feel.

I knew that God had chosen a husband for me. Generous Abraham will be my father-in-law and his miracle son Isaac will be my husband. Beautiful Sarah has recently died, so both Abraham and Isaac will be grieving still. Maybe I can help to comfort them both.

Hospitality. I never suspected where it would lead me.

Four

The Golden Calf

For the true story, see Exodus 24:12-18 and Exodus 32. The chapters in between are words God spoke to Moses while he was on Mount Sinai.

Sometimes I feel very inadequate and old. My brother Moses keeps climbing up and down Mount Sinai, but I stay at the bottom. He speaks to God, and I am left having to speak to the people. They are God's people, so I can't be too critical of them – after all, he chose them – but I know that I would far prefer to speak to God.

But this time, while Moses was away, I made a really bad mistake which almost caused the death of everyone in the camp, including me.[8] He was away for longer than I expected, and that was probably the reason everything went so badly wrong. Although he is my little brother, I have to say that Moses is an incredible man. He was deeply lacking in confidence when he came back from Midian, but that's not a problem anymore – to be honest,

---

[8] Deuteronomy 9:20

it seems to be more confidence in God than in himself, really. And spiritually he is so far above anyone I have ever met that I just don't feel as though I'm in the same category at all. Don't get me wrong, I would dearly love to be like him, and I find his attitude a great encouragement, but I just can't rise to his level.

And this incident just proved it all over again.

Moses went up Mount Sinai and I stayed down at the bottom with the people. Moses told the seventy elders God had chosen[9] that if they needed answers to difficult problems, they were to come to Hur or me. I suppose that meant we were in charge.

Mount Sinai[10]

Moses didn't go all the way up the mountain at first, just part of the way with Joshua, and there they stayed for seven days, waiting for God to tell him the right time to go the rest of the way up. Seven days was no problem,

---

[9] Exodus 24:1

[10] Sweet Publishing/FreeBibleimages.org: http://freebibleimages.org/illustrations/moses-golden-calf/ Slide 1

particularly with the presence of God being so obvious around the mountain. For six days there was a cloud, and then a fire came as well. It looked as if the top of mountain was burning. A truly amazing sight and one that made a deep impression on the people.

Then, from the flames, God called Moses, and he disappeared up into the cloud, heading up towards the fire that was the presence of Yahweh.

So Moses was gone and we were in charge. Everything went well for about the first four weeks. No important problems at all, just the normal day-to-day questions you get with such a large group of people. But then, all of a sudden, people started to notice that Moses wasn't there and to chafe at the restraints God had put on them. The fire was impressive, but even miracles lose their impact when they become everyday events. Manna kept coming every day – enough of a miracle to convince anyone for the rest of their life, you might think. But no, people started to discount God's work and to ascribe it to all the gods they had worshipped in Egypt. Those dead idols had been left behind with all the other rubbish in the hovels we had gladly abandoned, and Yahweh had proved himself to be the author of all the miraculous salvation we had enjoyed: plagues on demand, a dry path through the sea, and drinking water when we needed it.

Yahweh was still showing himself through daily manna (except on Saturdays) and the mountain still burned with fire, but the people wanted a god they could see. Miracles were all very well, they said, but they wanted a visible god to worship, and they hankered after all of the old gods they had worshipped in Egypt.

I know that sounds stupid – well, it is stupid – but we all seem to have a bit of "stupid" in us at times. The people started to show theirs and I was about to show mine too.

Trying to explain what you've done when it is so stupid is very hard. It's also hard not to try to excuse myself, but I'll do my best.

The normal ringleaders of whinging came to me, the very same ones who used to complain so much about the conditions in Egypt, yet now talk about it as if it were a holiday resort people would pay to visit.

"Make us gods," they said.

I said, "No. You have a God – Yahweh. He brought you out of Egypt."

"Moses brought us out of Egypt," they countered, "but he's gone. He went up the mountain and now who knows where he is? We need a god we can see."

I waved at Mount Sinai as it rumbled and glowed above us, "Look at the fire," I replied. "Your God burns the mountain with fire. You don't need to see God: see his work; eat the manna; hear the thunder from the top of the mountain."

"We want gods, or at least one god we can take around with us," said one; another said, "Moses led us out of Egypt, but we don't know what has happened to him;" to which a third replied grimly, "He probably got burned up."

The one thing they all agreed on was "We want a god we can see."

Hur decided to take a literal interpretation of Moses' words, and said this wasn't a matter for a legal decision, so he wouldn't be involved. That was all very well, but if we didn't do something, we would have idols springing up everywhere.

So they pestered me every day, becoming more demanding and aggressive each time.

Well, then; what should I do? How could I minimise the damage until Moses came back? Surely he should be back soon? By then, he had been gone for more than five weeks, but there was no sign of him or of young Joshua.

Anyway, two days ago, it all came to a head. Early in the morning, the delegation came again, with more hangers-on than ever, and a belligerent attitude all round. They were not taking "No" for an answer this time, and I knew that if I didn't do something to placate them, there would be idols and orgies all over the camp before nightfall.

That was when I made a really bad decision. Look, minimising trouble and harm is all very well as an idea – laudable, in fact. But when things are right or wrong, any toying with wrong is just plain wrong. Unfortunately I wasn't strong enough to say that – Moses would have – and I genuinely believed that what I was doing would work out for the best.

So I tried to give them a little of what they wanted, but still keep them on the right path. Needless to say, it didn't work. I thought I could just give in to a little bit of wrong and keep it under control.

I was wrong. Dead wrong.

Sometimes the only choice we have is to be either absolutely right or absolutely wrong.

I was absolutely wrong, and that's why I'm writing today. Don't follow my example. When God says "Do" or "Don't", then "Do" or "Don't" as he directs; don't try to mix God's ways with any other ways.

About 3,000 men died yesterday, and it could easily have been everybody had it not been for Moses. I feel responsible for it. I don't know what would have happened if I had stood up for God as I ought to have, but at least I would have a clear conscience now. Maybe God will have to get rid of other rebels as we travel to the land of promise, but maybe he will leave it up to us again as he did yesterday. I can tell you, it's really hard going around killing people for their sins when you know that you have made it easier for some to join in who might have stayed on Yahweh's side if you had set a better example as leader.

"Give me all of your gold earrings," I said, "and your wives', your sons' and your daughters' earrings as well, all of them. Bring them here and I will melt them all down and see what I can do."

I was still hoping that Moses would come back before they brought the rings, but no, they were amazingly quick, and soon I had piles of golden earrings lying on a mat in front of me, easily enough to make the sort of hollow image they wanted. After all, it had to be light enough to carry around with us.

And there were all the volunteers you could ever have wanted: helpers to make sure we had enough fuel for the furnace, helpers to light the furnace, expert helpers to make a rough mould, helpers with crucibles and ladles, helpers to sort the earrings and remove any that weren't pure gold. Helpers everywhere! But no helpers with any brilliant ideas of how to slow the process down until Moses returned. So the furnace swallowed up all of the gold, and after a while we had liquid gold glowing in several large crucibles. The mould was ready and heated, too, and little rivers of fire coursed down the sides of the mould as the crucibles were emptied into it.

℘

Large amounts of metal take a long time to cool, but by this time it was late in the day and the cold of the desert evening was descending to offer its unwanted help. Unwanted by me that is, but the image couldn't be finished soon enough for the eager onlookers. They even brought large quantities of water to help speed the cooling.

In an undesirably short time, the experts assured me that all the gold would have solidified and so the mould was broken off. I had to do some work with a tool to tidy up the image and make it look a little more like the calf they wanted, but then it was ready. The crowd had grown enormous – there must have been several thousand people there, cheering and shouting: "Here are your gods, O Israel!" Others answered them, "They brought us up out of Egypt."

What could I do? I had what I thought was a good idea and shouted, "Tomorrow will be a feast to Yahweh." It seemed better to allow them to treat this golden calf as a representation of Yahweh than to have them charge off into the worship of other gods. Some of those who had helped to make the calf looked at me as if they knew it wouldn't work, and didn't want it to work, either. But no-one argued out loud, so it was left that we would start our worship the next morning with burnt offerings and peace offerings to Yahweh.

You may be familiar with the expression "get it over with," and that was the attitude of many of the people the next morning. The offerings to Yahweh were treated by many as tedious necessities before the real business of the day could begin. I had tried to get people to worship Yahweh through the golden calf, but the people didn't really want that, and, of course, God didn't want it either.

As soon as possible, the feasting began and the feast rapidly turned into an orgy. Idol worship often seems to come with feasting – the sort of feasting that leads to drunkenness with singing, dancing and debauchery.

Worshipping the golden calf[11]

If only I had taken a stand and refused their demands! I had let them get completely out of control,[12] and what would the Egyptians say when they heard about this?

---

[11] Sweet Publishing/FreeBibleimages.org: http://freebibleimages.org/illustrations/moses-golden-calf/ Slide 7

[12] Exodus 32:25

"One God, Yahweh", had been Moses' constant refrain to them, but now, if there was only one god for this nation, it was a golden calf, just like the ones the Egyptians worshipped.

And then, just as all of this was unfolding, Moses came back. When I first saw him, he was standing on a ridge of rock, only a short distance above the raised platform on which the golden calf stood. He was taking in the situation: the golden calf, the kneeling worshippers, the frenzied chanting, the dancing and the excitement, and even from that distance I could see the anger that shook him from head to foot. He was carrying two small tablets of stone, and as I watched, he raised his hands and flung them to the rock, where they shattered, sending a shower of fragments down towards us. Such was the ferocity with which he flung the tablets to the ground that some of the shards landed amongst the closest of the worshippers, kicking up the dust and causing them to start in bewilderment. As they looked up, they saw Moses, standing only about thirty metres away and looking down on them like an avenging angel!

Such is the respect and awe that most people have for Moses (when he is there), that many of the worshippers immediately leapt to their feet and ran. Moses' anger is a frightening thing, and I could see that it wouldn't be long before I was its target. I didn't like the thought, but I was still thankful beyond words that he was back. Now everything would be alright.

It was too. Moses ran the last few metres down from his vantage point and began to seize some of the firewood that sat near the wooden platform with its golden idol. He saw me standing near and called, "Aaron, I'm glad you're there. Come and help me burn down this platform and destroy the image." Together we piled the wood under the platform and set fire to it. By this time, some Levites had come to help, while some of the bystanders had begun to question or argue. But Moses was in no mood for argument; he was giving instructions for action. "First we burn it, then we must grind it to powder, mixing the gold with the ash as much as we can. Then we give it to them to drink," he said grimly. He gestured to some of those who had gathered, "Bring more wood," he demanded. Some of those he commanded had been members of the complaining committee the day before, but they all obeyed when Moses told them what to do. Maybe that is how I should have treated them.

Flames hungrily consumed the platform, glowing fingers reaching up, twining and re-entwining around the golden calf as it gradually sank lower, until suddenly one corner of the platform collapsed and a shower of sparks billowed upwards as the calf rolled over and disappeared into the enveloping flames.

As the fire continued its cleansing work, I went through a very unpleasant interview with Moses. He asked me what had gone wrong, and what they had done to torture me to make me do such a thing.

After that, we went to look around the camp, and found that the destruction of the idol hadn't stopped the wider rejection of constraint. It was revolting. Drunkenness and all other sorts of self-indulgence were on show everywhere. Revolting and tragic. Without doubt, there were always many who were eager to lead the people in this direction, but the firm hand of leadership in godliness should have kept it in check. My hands had tried compromise, and evil loves compromise.

We returned to the centre of the camp and Moses asked for volunteers. He wanted men who were on Yahweh's side. The men who answered the call were people who were not involved in the feasting, nor had they joined in the degrading 'play' throughout the camp. It was a great pleasure to see our family members and close relatives coming forward until we had a large group of Levites who were willing to commit themselves to God, whatever the rest of the nation might do.

Moses gave us instructions. We were each to get a sword. That sounded grim enough, but no one argued because we already knew how God felt about idolatry and immorality. Moses told us to go through the camp, killing all those who were doing this evil: our brothers, our companions and our neighbours, even our children if necessary. So we went out through the camp, finding and executing those who were guiding the people away from God to idols and those who were leading the people into utter immorality.

Once the killing started, many who had been revelling in the opportunity to cast off restraint were suddenly sober and serious, and order was quickly restored. Even so, about 3,000 men were killed by the Levites that day. Those killed were not the only ones who were deeply involved in and committed to the breakaway. However, for the time being, the rest have escaped without punishment, and some may have learned their lesson. Others will merely wait quietly for another opportunity.

And now the golden calf is just a horrible memory. The troublemakers are back under control – for the time being.

Overall, it was good to have the opportunity to join other Levites in standing up for God. It gave me the chance to make it clear that my actions with the golden calf were just ignorance, folly and a lack of courage or wisdom. I never wanted anyone to worship any other god but Yahweh; I just thought a visible representation would help the people to worship our living, but invisible God. I was wrong, completely wrong. God wouldn't accept their worship of a calf, and allowing that sort of worship had led to other sins too. As usual, God's commands really are for the best.

Tomorrow morning, Moses is going up Mount Sinai again. God told him to make two new tablets of stone like the two that he had broken and to be ready to go up the mountain by morning.[13] God will write the testimony once more on the new tablets.[14] Once again, Moses will be gone, and guess who will be in charge again? Oh dear.

I hope I have learned my lesson and will do the job better. How long will he be away this time?[15]

---

[13] Exodus 34:1-2

[14] Deuteronomy 10:2, 4

[15] See Exodus 34:28 for the answer.

Five

Confessions of a Dancer-Snatcher

For the true story, see Judges 19-21, particularly Judges 21:16-25.

We knew it would have to come out sometime. Secrets have a habit of coming out when you least expect them to, and several times in the past we had discussed when would be the best time for us to tell the children to make sure they got the facts straight. After all, we didn't want them thinking that we weren't happy together – or that kidnapping a wife was a good idea!

Then, today, our oldest son Hushim came home from school and said to his mother, "Reuben said that his father calls Dad a 'snatcher'. When I asked him what he meant, he just looked mysterious and wouldn't answer. What could he mean?"

My wife says that she just smiled at him, tried to look mysterious herself, and said, "Wait until your father gets home, Hushim, and we will answer that together."

So, naturally, by the time I came in from the fields, Hushim was as beside himself with curiosity as a 12-year-old boy can be. And his two little sisters and two little brothers weren't far behind him either.

Literally, my foot was still in the air – I hadn't even set foot in the house – when he pounced on me.

"Dad, Dad, why does Reuben's Dad call you a 'snatcher'?"

My wife had made sure that she was there to see the interception, and she caught my eye with a crooked smile on her face. The time had come.

But I could still put it off for a little while longer.

"It's time to eat, Hushim," I responded. "After that, we might have time to talk about it. Otherwise, it might have to wait for tomorrow."

He started to complain, but then he looked up at me and saw that I was laughing, so he toned down the complaint just enough to avoid getting in trouble, while still making sure I realised that he desperately wanted to know the answer.

We sat down to eat and my wife and I found ourselves exchanging smiles a few times during the meal, helped along by questions from the little ones like, "What's a 'natcher' Daddy?"

Hushim corrected his little sister loftily: "The word is 'snatcher', you little silly."

"Well, why are you a 'snatcher', Daddy?"

My wife intervened with another smile, and I remembered that it was her smile that had first attracted me to her. "Just let your father eat his meal, dear. We don't want to snatch away his appetite, do we?"

" 'Natcher'-ally not," I responded.

Immediately after the meal ended, Hushim was at my side. "Are you ready now, Dad?"

"Yes," I responded. "Let's begin."

The bedding was all ready for the night, so I laid myself down on the mat on which two of the younger ones slept. The children quickly came and lay down beside me, and we all settled ourselves down comfortably with just a single flickering lamp giving us light. Now that the moment had actually arrived, I was feeling rather nervous. It was all very well to joke about things, but it had been a very difficult time, following on as closely as it had from an utterly catastrophic time. But I wouldn't go into much detail about that horrific drama with the children.

"We have never told you how I met your mother," I began, "so we're going to tell you tonight. And we need to start by telling you all that we are very happy together now, so how we met doesn't matter much to us anymore, but it was, shall we say – unusual."

As I looked around at the children, their eyes all gleamed in the dim light, and not one looked the least bit tired. Maybe if I drew the story out, the youngest ones would go to sleep. But now I had to start.

"Let me tell you a story. It's about a very sad time, fourteen years ago, when many, many people died, including both of my parents, all of my brothers and sisters, and most of the relatives I knew. When I was just twenty years old, there were some very big battles. Almost everyone in Benjamin died in those battles, which is why our towns are so empty now and we all have so much land to live on. I was in a group of 50 soldiers, and only two of us are alive now – all the rest were killed. Many thousands on the other side died also."

As I recited this bald summary, my hands began their familiar shaking, and I stopped speaking as the catalogue started to scroll through my brain as it always did: going through, one by one, how each of my fellow soldiers had died in those terrible battles against the other tribes of Israel.

My wife saw how I was feeling and started to say, "I think that we'll finish the story there for tonight," but I interrupted: "No, no. I can continue," and with a great effort, I did.

"When the battles ended, a few of us Benjaminites – only 600 – escaped to a place in the wilderness where we would be safe. I don't really know how I got there, but some of the older soldiers helped me to keep moving and not give up. Anyway, we stayed there for four bleak months, ending in the depths of winter. We almost starved. Then a deputation from the other tribes came to see us, and they spoke of peace. So we collected together our pitifully few goods, and set off for the land of Benjamin. When we arrived, we found a camp of soldiers acting as guards for 400 young women who were almost beside themselves with grief. They were all from a town in the north of Israel called Jabesh-gilead; apparently, the thirst for blood and annihilation had spread there too, and they were the only survivors of their town. All of the older women had been killed, and all the men too. Only these young women had been spared to be wives for us survivors of Benjamin. It was then that our true situation really struck home. We were being told that none of our womenfolk were alive. My parents had arranged with another local family for me to marry their daughter, but apparently, she was now dead, along with her entire family. And so was all of my family. It was a devastating time.

"We surviving men were all lined up on one side and the young women were all lined up opposite. There was a lot of quick pairing off – this man will marry this woman. But I was one of the youngest of the survivors, pushed down to the end of the line, and long before it came to my turn, there were no women left. About 200 of us still had no wife and no prospect of ever getting one."

I stopped speaking as I remembered the utter hopelessness I had felt. No family. No home. And now, not even the hope of happiness with a wife. We had been told that all of the other tribes of Israel had agreed that they would not give any of their daughters as wives to anyone from Benjamin, and there were no daughters of Benjamin alive to marry. I stared silently into the flame of the lamp for a few moments before my oldest son brought me back to reality with a jerk: "What happened then, Dad?" he asked, seriously.

"We returned to our homes and found everything in ruins," I answered and as I spoke, I saw again in my mind's eye the charred remnants of our home, with no traces of any of the family members who had waved me goodbye when I left. Over the years since, I have found a few places nearby with several bones strewn around and wondered, but I can't be sure.

"And then I started to build. All the woodwork had been burned, but the stone walls were still standing and it didn't take long to make the empty shell into a simple home again. The ongoing winter rain was a strong incentive! Some kind men from Judah and Ephraim were also travelling around helping, since most of the survivors were not builders or skilled in the things we now had to do. They helped us cart timber too, and I learned all I know about building from them. If only we had never fought them." Once again, I stopped and pondered, marvelling at the stupidity that had seen us, the men of Benjamin, fighting to protect vicious criminals from justice. It sounds ridiculous when it is put that way, and it was. Those murderers from Gibeah should have been executed at the start, but we didn't like being told what to do. We wanted to do it our way – and that's why so many died.

The lamp was still giving its warm yet feeble light, but the two youngest children had already succumbed to sleep. I wasn't sorry that they would not hear the whole story.

"As winter drew to an end," I continued, "our leaders met with the leaders of the other tribes again, and someone came up with a very, very strange suggestion to get wives for those of us who had missed out. Every year, there is a feast to God at Shiloh.[16] Lots of people go to it and there used to be celebrations and dancing. We Benjaminites who had missed out on getting a wife from the girls of Jabesh-gilead were encouraged to go along, so we did.

---

[16] Probably the Passover. God commanded attendance at three feasts every year (Exodus 23:14-17), but it seems that the Passover may have been the only one of these that was kept often during Israel's history. References to the feast are made in Joshua 5:10-11; 1 Samuel 1:3, 21; 2 Kings 23:21-22; 2 Chronicles 30:1-5, 26; 2 Chronicles 35:1, 18; Ezra 6:19-20; and even Luke 2:41 in New Testament times. 1 Kings 9:25 may suggest that Solomon kept the three feasts for some time.

"We hid in the vineyards next to a large open area just outside the walls of Shiloh where the dancers met. Apparently, it used to happen every year that the local girls had a special time of dancing, more or less by themselves. No guards, no supervisors, no chaperones, just hundreds of girls dancing and enjoying themselves together.

Dancing[17]

"We were all spread out through the vineyards which surrounded the dancers, and we stayed hidden, watching, for quite a long while. We watched the girls and each of us chose one that we liked the look of. I had my eyes on a tall, slim girl who danced beautifully and sang well too. But what caught my attention most was the way in which she smiled and spoke to the other girls. Of course, you can't really tell much about someone's character from just an hour or two of watching, but this girl seemed to be kind and gentle, whereas some of the other girls seemed to like

---

[17] "Dancer 63" by Erica B via Firkin
https://openclipart.org/detail/270849/dancer-63

showing off or pushing other girls around. Finally, once every man had chosen the girl he wanted, and we had made sure that each of us wanted a different girl, we got ready.

"The sun was going down by the time the signal was given. We all jumped up and climbed over the stone walls surrounding the vineyards and ran in among the girls as quickly as we could, taking them completely by surprise. Each man made a beeline for the girl he had chosen and grabbed her as quickly as he could. I made for that tall, slim, smiling girl, and did I have a fight on my hands! At first she acted as if she was going to run away, but then she turned around and slapped me – it was such a shock."

"I'm still sorry I did that," my wife interrupted. "I was behaving as badly as you were!"

Hushim looked at me wide-eyed and open-mouthed, then looked across at my wife. There was awe in his voice as he asked, "Was that you, Mother? Did you really hit Dad?"

"She did," I said, "but I managed to recover, snatch her away and bring her back here as my wife. Yes, I snatched your mother from among the dancers, and that is why Reuben's Dad calls me a 'snatcher'. Now it's time for bed."

Hushim was still looking from one to the other of us. His eyes were still wide, and his mouth still hung open.

"Hushim," said my wife, "it was very scary being stolen away like that. And my parents were very angry and complained to the judges. But what we didn't know was that the judges had been involved in arranging the whole terrible business, so they worked hard to convince my parents that everything was alright – as if it was quite normal for young girls to be stolen away and married out of hand when they went to the annual dance! Married life was very hard for your Dad and me for quite a while."

"And one more thing, Hushim," I added, smiling. "I do not recommend this as a way of getting a wife. For us, it has turned out well, but it would never have worked except for the fact that your mother is a wonderful and forgiving person."

"And one more thing, Hushim," my wife said, mimicking my words, "no-one would ever want to become a wife in this way. For us, it has turned out well, but it would never have worked except for the fact that your father is a very gentle and patient person."

My wife still has a beautiful smile.

Six

Achish – What Might Have Been...

For the true story, see 1 Samuel 21:10-15; 27:1-12; 28:1-2; 29:1-11.

Everyone near and far has heard of David, the mighty king of Israel. He is famous for many things, the earliest of which was killing a man from my home town. An astonishing specimen was Goliath – so tall he had to duck under every doorway in the city, even in my palace. But he wasn't noted for his airs and graces. Foul-mouthed and abusive, he was a fighter and a bully. It was no great loss when David killed him and dumped that enormous head outside the walls of Jebus.

What many people don't know is that David came to live in Philistine country on a couple of occasions. The first time was a bit of a fiasco. He came with a few hundred of his men and was seeking refuge from Saul, the crazy king of the Israelites at the time. Imagine that, a brave and brilliant leader having to escape from a king who didn't want his help! Amazing. Anyway, David came and some of my servants recognised him – they were retired soldiers.

His killing of Goliath had made a deep impression on them. Not only that, but they had seen him several times in the shambles that followed, and over the next few months. The thing which had upset them most, I think, was the humiliating songs of those young Hebrew women. "Tens of thousands." Naturally, these men were scared of him and didn't want him around, certainly not with the peerless sword of Goliath which he was carrying with him. Bringing that sword was probably not the wisest thing David ever did.

Young Knight in a Landscape[18]

---

[18] "Young Knight in a Landscape" by Vittore Carpaccio
https://upload.wikimedia.org/wikipedia/commons/thumb/0/0e/
Vittore_Carpaccio_-_Young_Knight_in_a_Landscape_-
_Google_Art_Project.jpg/713px-Vittore_Carpaccio_-
_Young_Knight_in_a_Landscape_-_Google_Art_Project.jpg

Never mind that though, David could see that the situation wasn't very safe and he started to act like a madman. I suppose he had seen Saul behaving like that often enough: dribbling and raving. That's why we called him Crazy Saul. If the rumours we heard were right, he would even throw spears at anyone who so much as looked at him while he was raving. Apparently, David had been his target a couple of times. David said that if Yahweh his God hadn't looked after him he would have been skewered like a boar.

But I'm getting off the track. David acted like he was a madman and I believed him. It's a little embarrassing to think how easily he tricked me. Anyway, I sent him away with all his men and he went back to sneaking and hiding in the desert areas of Israel.

We didn't hear anything much more about him over the next few years, until suddenly he turned up again – this time with his wives as well, and lots more men.

Well, I suppose he could really have taken over the entire city if he had wanted to, but he was all for peace, so I was happy enough to talk. Explanations made it clear that he was not crazy at all and never had been – his actions had all been a pretence to save his life. As I say, embarrassing.

What David also made clear was that he wanted to leave Israel permanently. Some of my staff didn't believe him, but I was confident that it was just jealousy. They didn't want someone as famous and brave as David around. I did. The other kings of the Philistines have always tended to push us around here in Gath. I and my ancestors have never been considered as important as the other rulers. Here was an opportunity to change that.

Imagine Gath as the sponsor and supporter of David, hero of the Israelites, now come to fight for us, not against us! And, of course, everyone would hear that this diplomatic coup was my doing. That wouldn't hurt either.

I handled the negotiations myself, and very successfully too. Not only did David stay, but he brought his family and those of all his men to stay in Gath with my army. A coup indeed! I can assure you that I slept more soundly in my bed at night with David and his men around, providing security.

Over the next two or three months, David helped to train my men. He was amazingly expert in all forms of warfare. Still in his twenties, he seemed to have a feel for leading men which I have never seen before. He could inspire men to follow him with just a few words, and he was always willing to speak to individuals. Even as a king, I felt I learned some things from him.

Proper Philistine equipment, real swords and helmets as well as armour and good tough sandals, were my gift of welcome to David and his men. It wouldn't do to have them looking like a rabble of Israelite cast-offs. In return, he shaped my men into a coordinated, disciplined fighting unit such as I had never seen before. I'm sure it made a massive difference the next time we met Crazy Saul in battle...but now I'm getting ahead of myself.

After about four months in Gath, David came to me and made a request. He was very nice about it – remarkably humble, really. Could he and his men go and stay in some other town, since he thought it wasn't very fitting for him to stay in the royal city with me! Wasn't that nice? Of course, I took some advice about this, and in the end decided to give him a town we had taken from Judah called Ziklag. None of my people really wanted to live there anyway, so it was just ideal. David made a buffer between us and the Hebrews, and started to attack them left, right and centre.

I was rather sorry to see him go, in fact. Even in such a short time, he had become like a son to me – such a contrast to my real sons. He was honest, open, reliable and, above all, trustworthy. If David told me something, I knew I could believe it completely.

So David moved to Ziklag, but I kept in close contact with him. I was starting to have the beginnings of a huge dream. Imagine taking over Israel completely with David's help. Imagine a Philistine kingdom, expanded to include Israel, with me in control. The other lords of the Philistines would have to recognise little Gath more and acknowledge me as the best person to rule such an extensive realm.

While in Ziklag, David started doing everything I could have imagined as necessary to bring the dream to reality. He attacked the areas of Judah and took lots of spoil. You should have seen all the loot! He showed it to me, so I had absolute proof of his work. He would never be able to go back to Judah now, not without Philistine help! But with it, he could take over and we could rule together. He also attacked the Kenites and the Jerahmeelites, both of whom were our enemies.

Sixteen months David spent working for me, but the end was tragic. In one piece of catastrophic meddling and monumental bungling, the lords of the Philistines demolished my careful plans. Success was in sight, and when I first heard that a showdown with Crazy Saul was inevitable, I was pleased!

Our army commanders had decided it was best to attack from the north, so all the army had to march from our comfortable homes up to the north of Israel. Naturally, I took David and his men with me. Well, if you don't know what stupid means, just listen to this. The commanders of the army saw David and his men, and straight away they went whinging to the other lords. "David this, David that, David the other." To sum it up, they were scared. Scared that David would turn on us in the battle and fight for Saul. Fight for the man who had used him for target practice more than once? The other lords might be stupid, but David wasn't. I knew that could never happen. David could be trusted.

I suppose it doesn't really matter now how stupid it was. But I still feel sad every time I think of it – which is often. My beautiful plan: Israel and Philistia combined, with David and me in control and those surly lords put in their place! All ruined.

History will record that David was sent away by the lords of the Philistines. History will tell that Crazy Saul was killed by our troops and we took over all of the north of Israel in the mayhem that followed. But history will also tell that David became king in the south of Israel, and that we have been fighting him ever since.

Oh, you lords of the Philistines – if only you had listened to me and not upset David, not told him he couldn't be trusted, not sent him away disgruntled and angry. Instead of being our friend, he is now our enemy – and where will the kingdom of Israel end up under his leadership?

If only....

Seven

Another Three Today

For the true story, see 1 Kings 3:1; 7:6-12; 9:10-24; 11:1-8, 26-40 and 2 Chronicles 8:11.

My name is Jeroboam, the son of Nebat from the tribe of Ephraim. I am one of King Solomon's construction managers, supervising the indentured workers from Ephraim. A while ago, we finished a big job closing up the gaps in the internal and external walls of Jerusalem. The city had grown so much under the reigns of David and Solomon that the original defensive walls of the old Jebusite city were not much use anymore. Thanks to our combined efforts, though, we now have a complete wall around the city, as well as various internal walls designed to help with the defence of the city should any breaches be made in the outer walls. The city is now without any obvious places to attack. I know that if I was considering attacking Jerusalem, I wouldn't bother!

But I don't want to talk any more about that.

Instead, although it's not really safe to do so – as quite a few people have found – I'm going to criticise King Solomon's latest behaviour.

You wouldn't believe what he is doing today.

Three more!

Already he has 722, but apparently, that's not enough for him. Egyptian, Moabite, Ammonite, Edomite, Sidonian, and Hittite women, as well as lots of Israelite women too. At times, the whole city seems to be full of King Solomon's women, and it made the construction work very difficult at times. It was hard to get the workmen to concentrate on the work – they were too busy watching the parading divas in their exotic clothes.

The problem started early in his life, but it started quite slowly – comparatively. I believe that Solomon only had a few wives when King David died, and Rehoboam his oldest son was born about a year before King David died. Of course, no-one grudges a king a few wives, and 5 or 10 or even 20 would have been alright, but once he started collecting them outright there was no stopping him.

Princesses were married to form political alliances. Some were almost taken as payment of debts and a form of tribute. Neighbouring kingdoms trying to ingratiate themselves with the wise young king were eager to throw their most beautiful girls in his face.

Even Pharaoh joined the mad rush to make a marriage alliance with Solomon, though he was in a more powerful negotiating position than most and had various requirements which Solomon had to meet before he handed over the prize. Solomon even had to commit to building a special palace for Pharaoh's daughter – but I suspect that there was also a preference there anyway. Of all his wives, I think she might be the one that Solomon likes best, although it's hard to be sure since he does his best to treat them all fairly equally – he has to, to keep their powerful relatives happy.

But thus far in his wife-collecting spree, Solomon has at least married them one at a time. This time, though, it's three. Three wives, all married at the same time. If you are a woman reading this, how would you like to be treated with that level of respect?

725 by nightfall today. But where will it all end? Nowadays, many a hard-working Israelite man can't find a good wife because their benevolent king has taken them all!

Solomon was a great king, but that was in the past. When he became king, it seems that he was amazingly wise and faithful to God. He even built the palace for Pharaoh's daughter outside the city of David because he said that the places where the ark of God had been were holy. I don't know what that says about Pharaoh's daughter!

Nowadays he is just wise, and it's a fairly crafty wisdom. Unfortunately, the dynasty of the house of David has become corrupt and cruel.

God gave us many laws, and some of them related directly to the king. Now I can understand that a king won't always want to be constrained by rules when he has a kingdom to run, but Solomon should have known better.

Let me just quote you the words Moses wrote about what a king should do, or more importantly, not do:

"...he must not acquire many horses for himself or cause the people to return to Egypt in order to acquire many horses, since the LORD has said to you, 'You shall never return that way again.' And he shall not acquire many wives for himself, lest his heart turn away, nor shall he acquire for himself excessive silver and gold."[19]

You couldn't get much clearer than that, could you? If I were king, I certainly wouldn't do what Solomon is doing. Each one of those rules he is breaking.

Horses: Solomon imports horses from Egypt. Hundreds and thousands of them. Do you know how many horses he has? He has stalls for 40,000 horses. Would you call that "many horses"? I certainly would. Now, I just wouldn't do that. It's wrong.

Many wives? Would you call 725 "many"? Sometimes he uses the distinction of "wives" and "concubines" so that it looks like he doesn't have quite so many. For a while, it worked to keep the number under 500 wives, but really: 508 wives and 217 concubines still adds up to 725. And it adds up to breaking God's laws.

Excessive silver and gold? Solomon has more silver and gold than everybody else in Israel put together, I think. Honestly, for him, silver is just like the stones that you might find lying around in a field. And every year, he gets 23 tonnes of gold. 23 tonnes! I suppose he needs to give all of those women lots of jewellery to keep them happy, but 23 tonnes is ridiculous. Some gold, carefully used to show the wealth and power of a kingdom and to help with religious ceremonies: that makes sense. But

---

[19] Deuteronomy 17:16-17

God's people Israel are not meant to measure their importance in gold. When Solomon started this massive collection, much of it was used to glorify Yahweh in his temple, but that need is long gone. Now the gold is all for him – and his wives.

Solomon's wives led him astray[20]

Most of Solomon's enthusiasm for construction now seems to be focused on building high places and other places of worship for his multitude of wives. In Israel, we now have places of worship for every god you've ever heard of. Solomon has wives from all around, and so now we have places to worship each of the gods from our neighbours all around. If you look out from Yahweh's temple across the Kidron Valley, you see a hill adorned with high places for Chemosh, Molech, Ashtoreth, Milcom and all the rest. I hear that Solomon spends quite a lot of time there now, and he's leading a lot of people away with him.

---

[20] Sweet Publishing/FreeBibleimages.org:
http://freebibleimages.org/illustrations/rehoboam-jeroboam/
Slide 4

It's just not right, bringing in all those foreign influences. All those foreign women virtually run the place! Israel should be for the Israelites. Israelite men and Israelite women. And our worship should be the worship of Yahweh, the God of our fathers. Maybe people are right when they say we should spice it up a bit. Many find the worship of these other gods a bit more exciting, so we have to make sure we don't lose the hearts of the people. We'll have to see about that. But our worship should be the worship of Yahweh.

You may wonder why I am bringing all of this up now, when I am one of Solomon's favourite supervisors. Well, it's like this: I am going to be the next king. I'm going to take over from Solomon instead of letting his foolish son Rehoboam lead us all to disaster.

How do I know that? Just last week, I was walking by myself on a road near Jerusalem, when a prophet of God called Ahijah came up to me. I'm not sure how he knew me, but I suppose I am quite famous because of my successful work. Anyway, he stopped me. He was wearing a garment that was obviously new, but he took it off and started to tear it into pieces. In the end, there were 12 pieces of material lying on the road, and he told me to take 10 of them because I was going to become king over 10 of the tribes of Israel. Since then, I have been thinking a lot about what he said, including his statement that the house of David had gone after other gods, and I have seen that it is clearly true. Not only that, but this repulsive collecting of wives is really at the root of the problem for Israel.

So, I've got to start getting ready to take over from King Solomon. I wonder what would be the best thing to do with all of those women?

At this rate, if Solomon reigns as long as his father David, he will end up with almost 1,000 wives and concubines! It's ridiculous. Shameful. Destructive.

Eight

The Widow of Zarephath

For the true story, see 1 Kings 17:8-24; 2 Kings 1:7-8.

He came with the twilight, as the sun sank below the horizon; a ball of orange fire sinking into the Great Sea. Filaments of cloud glowed scarlet, and the ethereal beauty of the sunset hid the barrenness of the landscape beneath. His clothes were simple but rough, and a belt encircled his waist.

Standing off to the side of the road, bent over and slowly collecting sticks as I was, I was hoping he wouldn't see me in the dusk, but he must have, for he called in a croaky voice, "Give me a little water in a cup. I need a drink."

Foreign sounding, I thought. I wondered where he came from. From the sound of his voice, he had not drunk for some time. Travelling? Or running away?

A widow collecting sticks[21]

At least we still had some water, so I straightened up and laboriously turned towards the well to get him some, but his voice stopped me: "...and bring me some bread as well?"

His voice reminded me of my husband's voice in the last few days before he died. Croaking. Weakening. Dying. So many had died of starvation and wasting disease during this terrible, never-ending drought. But what could I do to help? I wasn't so far off dead myself.

"I have no bread, nor anything baked at all," I said. "All I have is a handful of flour and ever so little oil in a jug. That's it." It was, too. I had measured the flour that morning, and it didn't quite fill my hand – even little Yeled might have been able to hold it in his small hand. As for the oil, no container I have could really gather the few remaining drops out of the jug I store it in. The only way to use it was to pour it out, with maybe a scraper to help, and that was just what I had planned to do. "I was just

---

[21] Sweet Publishing/FreeBibleimages.org:
http://freebibleimages.org/illustrations/elijah-widow-boy/ Slide 5

collecting some sticks to light a fire and cook a last meal for myself and my son," I added. "After that, we die." Poor little Yeled. I hope it will be quick. It has been months since we last got any flour, and I have been eking it out, giving as much as I can to Yeled, and hardly eating any myself. It all seems so unfair. All I want to do is to look after him, but to do so I must eat some of the food he needs, or become too weak to help him.

"Don't be afraid," he replied. "Go and do that – but make me some first, then make some for yourself and your son, because this is what Yahweh the God of Israel says: 'The jar of flour will not run out, and the jug of oil will not be empty before the Lord sends rain on the earth again.' "[22]

Sometimes when everything is going wrong and there seems no way out of a problem, exhaustion is actually a help. If I had been well-fed and strong, maybe I would have argued more and told him what I thought of his selfishness – fancy demanding that I feed him first! I had no way of knowing whether this promise of his was trustworthy or not. For all I knew, it could have been a heartless ruse to steal the very last of the food from our mouths. But I was tired. So tired. What he offered sounded unbelievable, but the mention of the God of Israel gave me pause. The God of Israel still has quite a reputation among the nations for some amazing miracles – although most of them were centuries ago. And anyway, I couldn't leave a wandering stranger without any food or hospitality. It wouldn't be right.

---

[22] 1 Kings 17:13-14

After fetching some water, I went and did what the visitor had said. A cake of bread for him, and then I went to make some for us. That was all it took to know that he was telling the truth. After I had popped his bread in our little clay oven, I peered into the jar – no more flour than there had been, but definitely no less either. This was amazing enough, but it was looking in the jug that was an overwhelming revelation to me. There had been so little oil that I needed a scraper to scoop it out, but as I gazed in wonder, it was clear that there was now enough oil in the jug that I would be able to pour it out when cooking our next meal. Our next meal. There was a wonderful feel to those words. No longer was life a foreshortened story in which I was writing the last few words – now there was hope.

Was the man a magician, or was this the work of the God of Israel? This became the burning question in my mind over the next few months. Religion had never been important in our house – my husband considered the gods of Sidon, particularly Baal, stupid and cruel. He was cautious about what he said in public, but when we were alone, his words were cutting. I remember his words on one particular occasion: "If she is the sort of worshipper Baal wants, then I don't want Baal as my god. She lies, she cheats, she steals, and now she murders anyone who stands in her way." This outburst was sparked by some news we heard about a massacre of prophets of Yahweh – organised by our own princess Jezebel, who was now King Ahab's queen in Israel. I couldn't disagree. Jezebel had never been a favourite of mine – more spoiled brat than regal queen, and the way she used to paint her eyes...but don't get me started. Jezebel is not a good advertisement for Baal.

But Elijah was a good advertisement for Yahweh. He kept his promises. He worked hard around the house. He cared for me and for my son − a widow and a fatherless child − without ever taking advantage of me or making the situation difficult between us.

Over the time he stayed with us, I learned a lot about the God of Israel, but still I had my doubts. Elijah was always talking about Yahweh; how powerful he was and how compassionate. But the drought continued. For sure, Elijah had power: we ate the evidence every day! But it seemed obvious to me that he could not end the drought, or surely he would have done so as he saw how much everybody was suffering. So was Yahweh really the one who was causing the drought? It seemed a cruel thing to do, although I could see Elijah's argument that it was not as cruel as the worship of Baal or Molech which God was trying to stop. I suppose that it was the worship of other gods that caused widows like me and fatherless children like Yeled to starve to death well before the rich and powerful even began to suffer. One long drought would be nothing, despite all the suffering it caused, if we could only learn from it and abandon the heartless and selfish habits spawned by the idols we worship.

So my doubts stayed with me, even though I saw the flour replenished every day, and used the miraculous oil in each new morning's cooking.

It was probably the only way to get through my doubting and teach me to trust God: Yeled died. In just a few days, he was transformed from a happy, smiling lad to a cold and pallid corpse. The eyes, which reminded me so much of his gentle father, were lifeless, and my reason for living was gone. I was completely alone in the world. I took out my anger and grief on Elijah and his God, complaining that it was God who had killed him because I was a sinner. In my grief, it seemed that God was punishing me for doubting him, and maybe he was – how could I know? Whether it was punishment or not, I cannot tell, but I do know that it was through my son's resurrection that I gained complete confidence and certainty in the God of Israel. Now, I praise Yahweh, the God of Israel and give thanks to him every day for life and food and everything.

You see, when Elijah raised my son, he finally convinced me that it was God who was doing all of the miracles. His urgent plea to Yahweh that Yeled's life and breath should return to him was so moving and so persuasive. It was truly Yahweh who gave me back my little Yeled. Joyful, laughing Yeled.

And then, one day, Elijah was gone. He went with the sunrise, early in the morning, as the sun began to stain the clouds with crimson. His upper room stands empty now, but the flour still multiplies, and the oil continues to flow. No rain has come yet, but the comfort of knowing that food will continue for Yeled and me until the rain does come, that helps me to rest in Yahweh, my God.

Nine

185,000 times 55

For the true story, see 2 Kings 19:35-36, 2 Chronicles 32:21 or Isaiah 37:36-37. For the background to the story, read the whole of each of these chapters.

Editor's note: This story has been translated from the ancient Aramaic into English and all units have been converted to metric units along the way.

It was a nasty shock when we woke up this morning and found them all dead. Half of the day it took before we could make a reasonable estimate of the number of dead bodies and as the numbers mounted through the morning, they numbed my brain. When the tally was complete, it took my breath away and a voice kept saying in my head, "This can't be real!"

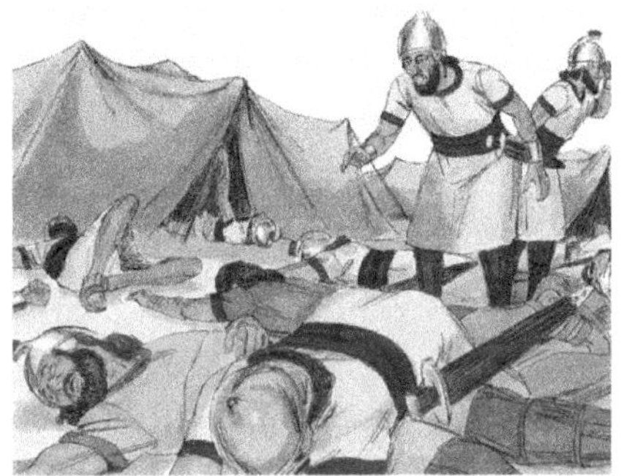

They were all dead men[23]

But it was real. There was no doubt about it. 185,000 corpses, and I was the one who had to deal with them. Why, you may ask? Well, unfortunately, I am the chief undertaker in the Assyrian army. They call me "Dumaya".[24] My job is to make sure that any of our soldiers who die in battle receive a decent burial, with the correct jugs, dishes, food, tapers, and all the rest of it. In short, we give "light to your departed" as tradition requires. And I already knew that in this disaster, it just couldn't be done.

On an ordinary day with no fighting, we have about four people die for each 100,000 men in the army and my staff can easily cope with that without needing my input. Before today, our army here at Libnah[25] was about 200,000 men since we are seriously trying to expand the

---

[23] Sweet Publishing/FreeBibleimages.org:
http://freebibleimages.org/illustrations/020-hezekiah-assyrians/
Slide 20
[24] Angel of Death
[25] Isaiah 37:8

empire. Battles can kill many more, and on disastrous days, we can have up to around two or three thousand soldiers killed. This can require some really hard work and ingenuity in disposing of our dead sensitively. Much more disastrous days happen to our enemies quite often, so I am quite proficient at swiftly disposing of large numbers of dead enemies – a task that requires no sensitivity at all.

But this time it was most of *us* who were dead. By the middle of the day, no-one wanted to eat because of the smell. I didn't bother telling everyone that it would get much, much worse before it got any better.

If we have 15,000 men left, and no-one else dies, each of us will have to bury about twelve and one third men. Our ordinary burial methods (when on active service) involve digging out 1.5 cubic metres of soil for each body. For each of us to bury more than 12 people, each of us would need to move more than 18 cubic metres of soil. Do you know how long that would take? I do – it's my job – it would take about 90 hours of work, given the soil we have here. Half a day more than a week. *Oh dear.*

Clearly that won't work. By the end of tomorrow, the smell around here will be so utterly unbearable that no-one will be staying to dig anything. There must be another way.

There's nobody else I can ask. The job is mine and so the ideas must also be mine. I was given this job because when difficult problems arise, I can solve them. An army needs that sort of man when unexpectedly high casualties occur, otherwise morale starts to slip. Proper respect must always be shown to our Assyrian dead. The dead of our enemies don't matter, of course, but our own dead must be buried quickly and honourably.

So now everyone is waiting for my instructions.

Since burying them all wouldn't work, what about cremation? We don't use cremation normally, but this was a special case and I was sure I could get the priests to agree without too much trouble. I called my 2IC[26] and told him to take two thousand men and start collecting logs from the nearest stand of trees.

"Yes, sir," he responded. "How many do we need?"

Oh dear. I needed more data. At times, we have had to destroy large numbers of enemy corpses, and fire has been found to be quite effective. It cleans up the mess and generates fear amongst the surviving enemies. But it also uses a lot of wood. *Think now, think.* I turned away from him and struggled to remember the details, and finally had enough to go on. It takes about twice as much wood to burn as there is body to destroy. So, if each body weighs about 55kg on average, that makes 110kg of wood per man...20 million kilograms.

We each need to cut, carry and burn almost 140kg of wood. Ah well, that should be easy enough, let's get on with it. I started to turn back to give the answer, but in the back of my mind, I had a niggling feeling that the answer didn't make sense. And then I saw the problem: I was wrong by a factor of ten. Not 140kg but 1,400kg of wood each, or about two 15m high trees. Each of us. Cut down two trees almost half a metre in diameter and chop each into pieces small enough to transport, bring it all back here and burn it along with the rapidly decomposing bodies. All within 24 hours or so. We Assyrians may have been the first army to be fully equipped with iron weapons, but we certainly

------

[26] Second In Command

don't carry around enough saws and axes for 15,000 of us to have one each. So that wasn't going to work either, but at least it would give the men something to do – at the moment, they were all stumbling around as if in shock. They probably were in shock. I certainly was. 185,000 corpses.

"Bring me 30,000 trees," I said wearily, and dismissed him without waiting to see his jaw drop, already having moved on to seeking the next possibility.

Maybe lime? I didn't really know much about this, but I had heard that powdered limestone could slow down the decomposition of bodies by drying them out. How much? No idea. Where would we get it from? No idea. Not worth pursuing.

Just cover the whole area with dirt? Not digging individual holes, just piling up some dirt over the entire area. Unfortunately, the bodies were spread out all around the city, so that wasn't really going to be any easier. How about digging big pits, putting thousands of bodies in each and then filling each of them up with dirt? By this time my mind should have been working smoothly like a well-oiled catapult, but it wasn't. 185,000 corpses. It slows down your ability to think clearly. The one thing that was becoming clear was that – *No! Stop It!*

Don't panic. Keep thinking.

Big pits, 12,000 men digging, while 3,000 brought the bodies to the pits. 500 diggers in each of 24 pits, and each pit would need to hold...er...7,700 bodies. If we want them to be under the ground, that means we need to remove about 450 cubic metres of soil for each pit and then pile it back on again after we put the bodies in. That's about one cubic metre per digger which should take about five hours. Plonk the bodies in the hole and quickly put the soil back in an hour or two, and we are all finished in under a day! I chewed my lip thoughtfully, maybe this wouldn't be so bad after all. But, first, check the details one more time before we make any commitment to this.

All of my estimates had been ignoring any possible complications, so what extra details might slow us down? That was when it struck me that the city we were camped around might have something to say about this! If they came out and helped, that would be good, but it was much more likely that they would notice something was up in our camp, see us handling dead bodies and digging trenches and so on, and send out a few raiding parties. After that...well it wasn't hard to guess that we were going to end up trying to dig holes with men from the city attacking us; carrying corpses while the populace from the surrounding areas tried to knock the stuffing out of us.

Could we spare enough men to protect the rest as they worked? After all, there were only a few thousand men in Libnah and they wouldn't commit them all to a fight – we would still outnumber them if we formed up. But we would be spread all around, in ones and twos collecting bodies, and in larger groups digging pits. Even if we overcame this setback, there was still the question of where we would put the soil while the cadavers were being put in the pits ready to be covered over. Everything would conspire to slow us down, and now, to top it all off, the sun was coming from behind the clouds. I could almost feel the smell getting suddenly worse.

How many bodies could we fit in the cisterns? There were several cisterns around the city. Our engineers had investigated them to make sure they were clean and to see whether they could provide us with enough water. Of course, they couldn't – no city wants to provide an easy supply of water for attacking forces. Large cisterns are always constructed inside city walls. Even so, the cisterns were relatively large and totalled almost a million litres – enough to last our original army for up to nine days if we were careful – but we had more than ten million litres of bodies to dispose of. Whatever way I looked at it, I couldn't see a way forward.

Wells – not enough volume there either.

Lakes – the bodies would all float as they decomposed. A lake full of bloated floating "conquerors"? Not exactly a good presentation of overwhelming Assyrian power.

I'm afraid we didn't have any choice. In the end, we had to walk away and leave the bodies to rot. Even the Assyrian army can be bested sometimes.

Women of Assyria, I failed you. I gave no "light to your departed".

I only hope the king won't mention this in his annals....

Ten

El or Bel?

For the true story, see 2 Kings 24:1; 2 Chronicles 36:6-7 and Daniel 1-2

The last two years have been tumultuous years and I would never have got through them without Yahweh, the only mighty, living God. My name, 'Daniel', acknowledges God in its last syllable, 'El', and this reminder has been a great help as my world has fallen apart around me.

Just two years ago, I was living a relatively comfortable life with my family in Jerusalem, but now, here I am in Babylon at the beck and call of my "supervisors" and always in danger. In danger, that is, if I forget that God is in control.

I could make this a very emotional tale, because I have seen many horrific things during those years, but it is probably best to be as dispassionate as possible.

Judah is a small kingdom and, because of its location, is liable to be caught in the middle when powerful nations collide. And that is what happened to one of the best kings we ever had, Josiah. About five years ago, he was killed in a battle with Pharaoh Neco,[27] who had been on his way to fight the Babylonians. Josiah was a good and righteous king, and his death was a tragedy for the nation. I was only thirteen years old at the time, but I remember the outpouring of grief it provoked. Jeremiah the prophet even wrote a very moving psalm recalling Josiah's exemplary work as a king. If only his sons had followed his example.

The people of the land immediately made his son Jehoahaz king, but only three months later, Pharaoh Neco returned and took him away to Egypt. No great loss, as he was nothing like his father and was not a good king.

Neco made Jehoahaz's older brother Eliakim king instead and renamed him "Jehoiakim". Now names don't mean much to most people, and those two names mean much the same thing anyway, but Jehoiakim would have been a bad king whatever his name.

Then two years ago, Nebuchadnezzar became king of Babylon, and one of the first things he did after he was crowned king was to come to Judah. His army surrounded Jerusalem and entered the city after a short siege, killing, maiming and mutilating. Many were taken away into captivity.

At one stage, Jehoiakim himself was in chains ready to be transported to Babylon, but he woke up to the seriousness of his situation and acted with abject humility. He promised to serve King Nebuchadnezzar faithfully, and his obsequious submissiveness won him a reprieve.

---

[27] Also spelled "Necho" and "Nechoh".

But only him. The rest of us were led away bound with heavy chains, suffering as many beatings as it took to convince us to obey whatever instructions we were given.

I don't know whether it's true or not, but some of the older men have said that Nebuchadnezzar picked out all the people he thought would be most likely to cause trouble and took them into captivity: nobles, princes, leaders, the intelligentsia and anyone capable of organising others. I'm told he even demanded the schooling results from across the country and took all the top students with him back to Babylon. An army with no leadership is dangerous only to its own side.

Then he made sure that none of these young men would ever raise any children to rebel against Babylon. It was just as God had predicted to an earlier king, Hezekiah, about a hundred years ago.[28] Hezekiah hadn't worried much about the prediction because he knew it wouldn't be in his time, but we were the targets of the prophecy and couldn't dismiss it quite so blithely.

But life is what you make of it once you've been given the clay to work with, and no task is ever beyond us when God is with us.

All Babylon turned out to welcome King Nebuchadnezzar and his army, celebrating a well-deserved victory over inferior foreigners. The throng of soldiery had paused outside the city to make sure that all the victorious fighters were cool, clean and splendidly presented, and the magnificent streets we passed through

---

[28] Isaiah 39:5-8

were lined with cheering men, women and children welcoming the returning heroes.

We were the centrepiece of the parade, presented to be ridiculed in our chains and accumulated dirt. The cream of Judah's nobility and youth – the filthy representatives of a subjugated nation.

Bitterness is easy to cultivate, but never leads to a better life. God wants higher things from us and shows us what he expects through people like Joseph, my own personal hero from among all the patriarchs our scriptures describe. I have always wanted to be like Joseph, and that is a tall order indeed. He was seventeen, just my own age, when he was taken into Egypt as a captive, so it's an obvious link to grasp at and be inspired by.

The king's plan was to teach all the young captives from Judah to be good Chaldeans. Our teachers were to tell us hesitantly that we were probably clever enough to learn Modern Science, then spoil us rotten with food and dazzle us with science. At the end of the process, we should have a healthy regard for the brilliance of Babylon and its gods and a scornful disdain for the God of our fathers.

Of course, what they didn't realise was that most of the lads already had a scornful disdain for the God of their fathers, while the few of us who didn't weren't going to learn it any time soon.

The first step was to take away our names that acknowledged El Shaddai, or Yahweh, the God of our fathers. For me, that meant my name Daniel was to be replaced by the name Belteshazzar, a name which acknowledged Bel, the god of King Nebuchadnezzar.[29] In some ways, a name is unimportant, but in this case I was being given the name just to make the point that the king's gods were more powerful than the God of Judah. So I prayed to the true God and asked for his protection. I didn't look for a confrontation about it, but I never used the Babylonian name, nor did I respond when it was used to me. For me, it could never have been right to accept the new name, and God answered my prayers – I never got into trouble over it. My friends were also given new names, but they decided that it didn't really matter what names they were called and that they would prefer to make a stand for God on more important matters, which we were all sure would come soon enough. As a result, they are known by the names Shadrach, Meshach and Abednego most of the time, although I still prefer their Hebrew names Hananiah, Mishael and Azariah.

Sure enough, the king's menu brought on the confrontation we had expected. King Nebuchadnezzar is a rich, pagan king, and his tastes in food reflect this. He wanted us to share the food, but as Jews, we are bound by God's rules regarding clean and unclean food, and must not eat any blood. Exotic and fascinating the king's food might have been, but I was utterly convinced that it would include food that God would not want me to eat. The four of us discussed it and agreed that I should talk to Ashpenaz and seek an exemption. After praying, I made an appointment to see him in his office, since it was going to be easiest if there was no-one else around.

---

[29] Daniel 4:8

First I had to convince Ashpenaz that I was serious. He couldn't believe that anyone could fail to appreciate the gracious compliment of being singled out by the king to share his rich food! Multitudes would be willing to kill for such an honour. God helped me to explain it effectively, and that led to the next complication. Ashpenaz wanted to know why I and my friends cared so much about this when the other young Jews from Jerusalem all seemed very eager to eat the king's food. Now that was a more difficult question to answer honestly without the answer reflecting too critically on my fellow Jews. Taking a young man away from his family and encouraging him to abandon all familiar restraints will lead most to abandon their religious commitments, assuming that they had any in the first place, but the truth was that most of my fellow Jews had little interest in Yahweh anyway. Eventually Ashpenaz was able to be convinced that we had a commitment which we must keep whether others did so or not. This led to the most difficult part of all: would he permit us to eat food that Yahweh would be happy with rather than the food the king wanted us to eat? Ashpenaz was very doubtful. He was certain that the king's food was better; well, of course! His mind could not even begin to consider the idea that eating vegetables would make us healthier and stronger. Without God's blessing, there is no way I could ever have convinced him, but with it, we were able to agree to a 10-day trial.

Eating only vegetables[30]

Those were interesting days. I was sure that we would do very well on a diet that pleased God, but would the difference be great enough, and would it show quickly enough? Of course, I couldn't be sure, but I did have a lot of confidence that God would make sure we looked much better very quickly if he wanted us to be able to obey his commands. We had not been fed very well on the forced march to Babylon and were not in very good condition, but sure enough, after just a few days, we four were looking and feeling much better, while the others were still looking much the same.

We were examined first by Ashpenaz, and then by the chief cook, a doctor, a food scientist, a religious expert and the king's dietician. I've never felt more examined in my life! They even gave us some memory and mathematics tests to make sure, and seemed rather surprised by the results.

---

[30] Sweet Publishing/FreeBibleimages.org:
http://freebibleimages.org/illustrations/daniel-food/ Slide 10

In the end, they all concluded that we were very healthy, which we already knew. But the next step made us exceedingly unpopular with the other students: all their rich food was taken away from them and instead they were given vegetables and other foods that Yahweh has told us are clean.

El or Yahweh, who my name declares to be my judge[31] won the health competition. It shouldn't really be a surprise that he knows what is best for the human body – after all, he designed it!

℞

We slowly got used to our new conditions in Babylon. King Nebuchadnezzar put us in his best university, assigned us the best available professors and experts in all the areas he wanted us to learn and gave us the normal time – three years – to finish our qualifications. Of course, we did have one disadvantage – none of this education was to be in our mother tongue, Hebrew.

I have never been quite sure whether King Nebuchadnezzar originally wanted us in his court as trophies or because he felt that Babylon could learn something from foreign countries. Whatever it was, he certainly treated us well. Babylon was the centre of academic excellence at that time and we went to the best university available. If you like, it was the best college or university in the world.

Our performance was to be reviewed every year and our supervisors made it very clear that, while they didn't

---

[31] Daniel probably means "God (El) is my judge".

expect us to do quite as well as the native Babylonian students, we would be in serious trouble if we didn't get reasonable results.

Many would call it an honour, and it certainly was a marvellous opportunity to learn all of the wisdom and science that a powerful empire could teach. In the end, however, we found it a little disappointing because the knowledge that they promoted ignored established facts and tried to fit the world into their own predetermined views. Our lecturers *knew* that their society was the best in the world and that they, personally, were the cleverest and best representatives of that society. Unfortunately, the fact that they had been told these things from childhood meant that they were unable to open their eyes to obvious facts. Because Babylon had defeated Judah, they had little but contempt for Judah. Some of us exiles had more open minds, however. We knew a God who had not only predicted this defeat, but had specifically caused it to happen as a punishment for national disobedience.

When you are blessed to know a God who can consistently foretell the future accurately, you listen to the other things that he says too – if you are wise. So we knew that the creation and maintenance of the world came from one God, Yahweh. And we knew that if there were questions about what would happen in the future, Yahweh could answer them.

Yes, we were able to walk a balanced path. We revelled in the learning of mathematics and other items of science where they fitted with God's view of the world as we knew it from our scriptures and the world around us. But when they told us their peculiar stories about creation, the flood, witchcraft, the interpretation of dreams and the significance of the location of maggots in a decaying liver, we decided to listen to the maker first – after all, he is the one who knows! "Science" is not all it's cracked up to be. We watched sadly as many of the young men from Judah showed that they weren't so clear in the matter as they started to accept the Babylonian religion, science and so on. The names of Babylonian gods littered their conversations and the God of Israel became a symbol of failure to them. Even the success – God's success – with our diet couldn't convince them that they should think again.

Nevertheless, it didn't take long before Hananiah, Mishael, Azariah and I were all getting results at the very top of our classes, despite the language difficulties. Although my friends were only young, wisdom just oozed out of them because they were familiar with the wisdom of Yahweh. Their minds soaked up the literature and language of Babylon as water soaks into a sponge, and the wisdom that they could mix with their new knowledge made them stand out in all of the classes, from Aramaic literature to the interpretation of dreams, from mathematics to palace etiquette.

At our first annual review, after just one year of education, Nebuchadnezzar read reports of our performance. All of the student captives were called before the king, along with various professors and Ashpenaz the chief of the eunuchs. It was our first visit to the king's throne room.

Ashpenaz told me later that when Nebuchadnezzar scanned the results, he couldn't believe what he saw. The list included the results of all of the students in our year level from the entire university, and we captives were identified on the list with a special symbol. Nebuchadnezzar looked at the results and tried to work out what had gone wrong. You see, at that time, the university had a set of standard subjects that everyone had to do for each course, but you could also do extra subjects from other courses and higher year levels and get lots of bonus marks – as long as you passed and were doing well in the mandatory subjects. We did a lot of extra subjects. Imagine King Nebuchadnezzar's surprise when he saw four of his trophy captives at the very top of the results list, with scores that were ten times as high as any of those achieved by his native Babylonian students! It was a wonderful poke in the eye for his gods, although none of us ever told him so. While I never show reverence for King Nebuchadnezzar's gods, I never show contempt either. I want him to learn for himself that Yahweh is so much better than his gods. He is learning – slowly.

The king reviewed the results and asked Ashpenaz what should happen next with our education. Ashpenaz replied that with those marks, our education was finished! We had passed the accumulated number of marks needed to graduate.

There in the throne room, the king asked all of the captives lots of questions, but he concentrated on us four. It was clear that he wasn't completely convinced about these results. But we were guided by God in our answers, and with his help and the wisdom from our scriptures, we were even able to answer some of his pet questions, problems that none of his enchanters and astrologers had ever been able to give him convincing answers for. That impressed him, but he still got his Chaldean experts to ask us all sorts of questions from a huge range of subjects to see whether they could trip us up. We did our best to make it clear that our wisdom came from Yahweh. In the end, he and his experts were convinced, and so the four of us graduated and King Nebuchadnezzar appointed us to positions in his palace. We even stood in his presence in the throne room itself from time to time.

Another victory for the God of Israel.

King Nebuchadnezzar is a little inconsistent. He is obviously a brilliant commander in battle, but sometimes he is quite impulsive and acts without thinking things through very carefully. He always has his Chaldeans and wise men available to give him advice, but sometimes he finds them frustrating and self-important.

Yahweh knew all about this, and he used it to get a message directly to the king. One night King Nebuchadnezzar had a dream. As usual, he asked his Chaldeans for an explanation of what it meant, but on that particular morning he was in a perverse mood and asked them to explain the dream without him telling them what the dream was. If they had handled the situation carefully, they might have been able to gently convince him to describe his dream, after which it would have been easy for them to follow their dream interpretation manual. Instead, they tried to throw their weight around and tell the king what to do. That was always going to be dangerous, and in this case, it would have been fatal for all the wise men of Babylon – including me – if the God of Israel hadn't had everything firmly under control.

The first that I heard about it was when Arioch, the captain of the king's guard, came looking for the four of us to take us to the prison, where all the wise men were to be executed. I was the only one in our rooms at the time, so

I found out what was going on and managed to talk Arioch into letting me go in to see the king. After a while, the king agreed to give us one night extra;[32] if we could give him the explanation of his dream in the morning, all would be well, but if not, our heads would roll with everyone else's.

I hurried back to our rooms and found Hananiah, Mishael and Azariah waiting for me there. They had heard news of the king's dream and were very worried. Of course, none of us knew then that God had arranged this so that he could get the right interpretation directly to the king, while at the same time promoting in Babylon some people who served him – us four.

So we set about praying to God for answers. The others couldn't understand how I could be so sure that God would give the answers we needed, and I didn't really know how to explain it to them. God is God, and I know that I can trust him. That was really all I could say. Faith is hard to explain, and I can't have faith for anyone else. Of course, my friends were certain that God *could* do this, but they weren't quite so sure that he *would* do it. For some reason, they seemed to have more faith in praying that God would give *me* the answer, so that was what they did.

Anyway, the God who gives wisdom answered our prayers and showed me a vision that night. I saw the king's dream and what it meant. There was no need for the *Complete Manual of Dreams* that the Chaldeans use, though I'm very familiar with it since it was part of our education and dreams have always interested me. Once I knew what

---

[32] Daniel doesn't tell us how much time was allowed, all we know is that the answer from God was given in a vision of the night (Daniel 2:19).

the dream was, I could see that the manual would not have given me the same interpretation at all and I knew that God's interpretation would be right. After a prayer of thanks, I went to Arioch with the news that Yahweh had shown the dream and its interpretation. Everything was being set up marvellously to show that Bel and the other gods of Babylon were nothing, but that the God of Israel was in perfect control.

King Nebuchadnezzar's dream[33]

In just a few minutes, I found myself before the king. He called me Belteshazzar, which I ignored, and asked me if I could interpret the dream for him. This was the perfect opportunity to make the most important point, but I knew that I would have to play it carefully and not take too long about it or I might never get the chance.

I told Nebuchadnezzar that no wise men, enchanters, magicians or any of the rest of them could possibly do what he wanted – but I watched his reactions carefully as I spoke. I could tell that he was thinking that I was

---

[33] Sweet Publishing/FreeBibleimages.org:
http://freebibleimages.org/illustrations/daniel-dream/ Slide 2

complaining to him just as his Chaldeans had done the day before, accusing him of being unreasonable and not playing by the rules. He was clearly becoming angry as I spoke, so I quickly moved to the really vital part of what I had to say: "...but there is a God in heaven who reveals mysteries, and he has made known to King Nebuchadnezzar what will be in the latter days."

And that was the end of that, really. I told him the details of his dream and gave him God's explanation of it. Once again, Babylon's gods were shown to be powerless, and Yahweh, El, my judge, was shown to have power.

Blessed be the name of God forever and ever.

I hope that King Nebuchadnezzar continues to learn his lessons!

Eleven

I'm Incistern on This!

For the true story, see Jeremiah 38:1-13 and 39:15-18. For some further background information, read Jeremiah 28 and 37:11-21.

I'm not really a brave man. Those officials really scare me: they have the ear of King Zedekiah and they whisper into it all the time. And they are vindictive.

So it was very encouraging today when Jeremiah came to me and gave me a message of hope.[34] He told me those brutes wouldn't get me. I suppose the rest of his message wasn't very heartening, but it did promise me life, so that was wonderful.

You see, Jeremiah told me that Jerusalem is going to be destroyed, but that I won't be killed when the Babylonians take the city. I will get to keep my life as a "prize of war" – whatever that means. I guess that I will be going into captivity to Babylon, but I don't really know.

---

[34] Jeremiah 39:15-18

I'll just have to leave that up to God. A bit scary still, altogether.

But God says I won't be handed over to Shephatiah, Gedaliah (the son of Pashhur, I mean – you know, the nasty one), Jucal and Pashhur (what is it about that name?), even though they would love to get their hands on me.

Now you may wonder what I did to get into their bad books. After all, everyone knows that they are dangerous people to cross, so surely I could have taken care. Well, I have certainly been very careful to keep a civil and polite tongue in my head over the past few years, despite the temptations otherwise. But this time....

These men, and the others that King Zedekiah my master surrounds himself with, are all very quick to demand loyalty and dedication to the cause of fighting the Babylonians, but they don't seem to see that it just won't work. Jeremiah is a prophet: he speaks words from Yahweh, and Yahweh has said that Jerusalem is not going to last very long. And not only that, but the destruction is coming because of people like Shephatiah and the rest; because of their lack of loyalty to God. What is the point of being loyal to unfaithful, cruel and vindictive people?

Anyway, as I said, I am not a brave man. A slave has to quietly take what he can get, and be very careful not to give offence to the wrong people. Yet that is just what I did: I upset Shephatiah, Gedaliah, Jucal and Pashhur. And not just a little, either.

Let me tell you the details, and you can decide for yourself whether I was brave, careless or just completely stupid. Myself, I don't think I had any choice.

CR

Jerusalem is under siege and has been for more than a year. The Babylonians sit outside, patiently waiting for us to starve, and that's exactly what is happening. Of course, they don't sit still all the time; their catapults keep slinging rocks at us every day, and from time to time they come with battering rams to attack the gates and the parts of the wall they think are weakest. In some parts of the city, we have had to knock down buildings beside the wall ourselves, and use the rubble to strengthen the wall.[35]

But it's not worrying about the walls or gates that keeps you awake at night. No, it's the hunger that gnaws at your stomach and wakes you from dreams of succulent steaks and fabulous feasts. And it's hunger that prompts people to desert to the Babylonians.

Now Jeremiah has been telling people for years that Jerusalem will be defeated by Babylon.[36] And ever since the Babylonian army came, he has been telling the leaders to surrender,[37] but the big, brave leaders don't want that to happen. They have a strange certainty that God will protect Jerusalem because of the temple[38] – the very temple that they despise and treat with contempt. So they blame Jeremiah for people deserting to the Babylonians.

It was after one of Jeremiah's speeches to the people that they got all upset. Of course, they weren't there

---

[35] Jeremiah 33:4

[36] Jeremiah 25:8-11

[37] Jeremiah 21:9; 27:12

[38] Warned against in Jeremiah 7:3-15 and reported from a few years earlier in Jeremiah 26:9-11.

listening – they never do listen to God's word – but they heard reports of it afterwards, and when they did, they almost went crazy. Off to Zedekiah they marched and told him just how bad Jeremiah was and that he should be killed because he was a traitor and making everyone give up, etc., etc., etc. Well, they've tried that before and it hasn't worked, so this time they managed to drop a hint to Zedekiah that they wouldn't actually kill Jeremiah even though they thought he deserved it, and Zedekiah gave them permission to do what they wanted.

But you see, they really did intend to kill him, just slowly, not straight away. So they dragged Jeremiah down into the bowels of the palace to the place called the court of the guard, where Prince Malchiah had his own private water supply cistern. It was easily big enough to put someone into and deep enough that no-one would be able to climb out of it. Now this was in the middle of summer, and all of the useable water from the cistern had been used. All that was left was mud – you know how it collects in cisterns – and when they pushed poor Jeremiah in, well, of course, he sank in the mud.

Now Jeremiah is in pretty good condition, but he isn't that young anymore. He's been a prophet for about forty years and he's in his late fifties, but these young guttersnipes just pushed him in and left him for dead!

When I heard about it the next day, I was furious, but what could I do? Logic told me I couldn't do anything, but my mind kept insisting that I had to try. I tried to get out of it, but after lots of arguing inside, I was finally convinced that I didn't have any choice. I was walking up towards King Zedekiah's throne room when I met one of his guards. He's a bit of a friend of mine, Jehonathan is, and I asked him if I could speak to King Zedekiah. I confess that, by that time, I was starting to get cold feet. After all, complaining to a king about his friends is a dangerous game to play, but my mind kept insisting.

You may be wondering whether it's really that easy to get to see the king, and, to be honest, it normally isn't. But my friend was on his way to deliver a message to King Zedekiah and he told me to come along. At the time, Zedekiah was actually in the area near the Benjamin Gate of the city, hearing some legal cases or something. On the way there, I explained my mission to Jehonathan and he stopped in mid-step and looked at me long and hard.

"Are you mad?" he asked, quietly. "Being a champion of Jeremiah is not the way to fame at the moment."

"I know," I said, "but I can't just let them get away with it, can I? I like Jeremiah and he really does seem to tell the truth from Yahweh. And I don't like seeing these young upstarts picking on a man of God who's twice their age."

"Hmmm," he mused, as he tapped the rolled-up message against the shaft of his spear. "Hmmm. If Zedekiah is letting his friends persecute Jeremiah, I don't think he's likely to listen to a servant like you."

"I have to try – it's just not fair."

"Well, it's your funeral, I suppose," said Jehonathan, and we walked on. I wished he had chosen a different idiom; hoped he wasn't going to be right.

We walked on and joined the crowd, and I started to think exactly what I was going to say to the king. After a few minutes, the case finished – I think it was an accusation of stealing food – and a man was dragged away in chains.

Then my friend, Jehonathan, moved towards the king, holding up his message, and I followed close at his heels. He handed over the message to the king, who started to open it, but then paused and looked enquiringly at me. My dark skin tends to attract attention here in Jerusalem – there aren't many of us Ethiopians around.

"He wants to talk to you about Jeremiah," said Jehonathan.

The king started and looked around him quickly. A guard standing nearby had also reacted and was looking interested.

"Irijah," said Zedekiah, beckoning, "go and make sure that the prisoner for the next case is ready."

Irijah moved away towards the guard-room of the gate and Zedekiah seemed to relax a little. "What do you want?" he asked me.

While standing in the crowd, I had worked out a fine-sounding speech that would convince King Zedekiah to free Jeremiah, but standing there before the king, I couldn't remember any of those beautiful words at all. "My lord, Shephatiah, Gedaliah, Jucal and Pashhur have done evil in throwing Jeremiah into Malchiah's cistern. He'll die of hunger down there in the mud. There's no bread left in the city, and sure as eggs is eggs, *they* won't be lowering down any bowls of soup for him."

Zedekiah looked around again, but there was no-one nearby listening. It's amazing how sometimes you can be almost alone in a crowd. "So that was what they planned," he said, drumming with the fingers of his right hand on his knee, and not looking very pleased. He leaned forward and said to me quietly, "You're Ebed-melech, aren't you?"

I nodded, amazed that he knew my name. King Zedekiah is really quite a nice person if you keep him away from his friends... but a man chooses his friends.

"I think you are right," he continued. "I thought they would just lock him up, but I should have known better. Alright, take three men – Jehonathan here can get another couple of men to help you; then get Jeremiah out of the cistern as quickly as you can. Preferably before my friends hear anything about it." He looked over his shoulder and saw Irijah returning with an unhappy-looking prisoner. "Go now," he said urgently, "and, Jehonathan, choose your helpers carefully. Don't tell anyone else what is happening until you have Jeremiah safe. Give him a room in a quiet area of the court of the guard – out of the dungeons."

By this time, Irijah was almost upon us, and Zedekiah looked at us almost apologetically before turning back to him and starting to discuss the next case. Irijah was looking at us curiously, but it was a curiosity tinged with anger, as if he somehow guessed what we were doing and didn't like it.

Jehonathan and I turned and walked towards the palace, and on the way, I asked him, "Who is Irijah, and why is he so interested in Jeremiah?"

"Irijah is a bitter enemy of Jeremiah's," said Jehonathan, "and he would be rejoicing if he knew where Jeremiah is at the moment. Maybe he does. He's always carrying on about trying to get Jeremiah."

"Why does he hate Jeremiah?" I asked. Here was yet another enemy I could be making.

"Irijah's grandfather, Hananiah, was a prophet," Jehonathan answered. "A false prophet. A few years ago, he contradicted Jeremiah's prophecies and said that the king of Babylon would be defeated and that all of the treasures taken from the temple would be brought back to Jerusalem within two years. It never happened, of course, but that wasn't the main point. A week or two later, Jeremiah said that he had been given a message from God saying that Hananiah had been telling lies while claiming they were prophecies from God. He said that Hananiah would die before the end of the year. And get this," Jehonathan stopped and grabbed my arm, stopping me too; "Hananiah was dead within weeks." He let go of my arm and we walked on as he continued, "Irijah blames Jeremiah. Funny really, because he keeps saying that Jeremiah is telling lies. Now I would have thought that if he didn't believe Jeremiah, he wouldn't believe he had the power to kill his grandfather either. Anyway, that's Irijah for you. Just a year or so ago, he managed to get Jeremiah beaten and locked up for a while,[39] but the king freed him that time, too. If you want my advice, I'd say watch out for Irijah and his friends. And Shephatiah and his friends too," he added dryly.

By this time, we were back at the palace, and Jehonathan went to the barracks where the king's guards live to fetch another couple of men to help, while I went to the storehouse where all the unused items from the palace are stored. I fetched some old rags and worn-out clothes from there, as well as some ropes, then I went downstairs towards the lowest levels of the palace, the parts that were

---

[39] Jeremiah 37:13-15

used as a prison. When I came to the deepest, darkest level, I found Jehonathan already there with a couple of his friends. I was glad that they had thought to bring torches, because without them we wouldn't have seen much. Even so, it was almost as if the darkness was swallowing up the fitful light of the torches, and the gaping hole in the floor seemed to ooze blackness.

A shallow gutter ran across the floor to the lip of the hole, with a few stones lying across it here and there, part of trying to keep rubbish out of the cistern, I guess. Beside one of the stones I saw what looked like a dead, desiccated rat, but it was hard to tell in the gloom. I didn't look too carefully. If these were the sorts of things flowing down towards the cistern, I wondered what items had got past the stones and were down there in the cistern with Jeremiah. More than just mud, I was sure. Again, I felt sorry for Jeremiah in his predicament, and angry with the men who continued to persecute him.

Jeremiah in the cistern[40]

---

[40] Sweet Publishing/FreeBibleimages.org:
http://freebibleimages.org/illustrations/jeremiah-cistern/ Slide 9

"Jeremiah!" I called, leaning over the dark opening and straining to see anything in the inky depths. I couldn't see anything at all, so I was rather glad when I heard his response:

"Is that you, Ebed-melech? Oh, thank Yahweh! I never thought to hear anyone's voice again. I had given up hope." His muffled voice sounded tired and there was none of the hope that normally enlivened his voice.

"You're not going to die this time, Jeremiah," I replied. "The king has sent us to get you out of there."

"How long have I been in here? It's so dark in here, I can't see whether it is day or night," he croaked. "What time is it?"

"It's the middle of the afternoon and as far as I can tell, you have been in there since yesterday morning. So let's get you out of there quickly."

I took one of the ropes and gave it to Jehonathan. "You take this rope with one of your friends and lower it down to Jeremiah."

One of the men looked a little doubtful in the flickering torchlight. "Is that really Jeremiah, the son of Hilkiah, down there?" he asked, and he looked at Jehonathan accusingly. "You never told me we were going to help him. He's a traitor, isn't he?"

"No, he's not," answered Jehonathan. "You can't believe everything you're told, you know. Who said he was a traitor?"

"Well, it was Pashhur and Irijah," the man replied. "They said he is encouraging people to betray us to the Babylonians."

"No he isn't," I said. "Jeremiah is just telling people that God says we are going to lose this war anyway and that if we give in quietly, we will be treated well, but if we keep fighting we will still lose and everything will be worse for everyone. That's not being a traitor, that's trying to help."

"Yeah, well," said the other, "I'm finding it a bit hard to tell the difference. We're in the army to fight, and he's telling everyone to give up. That doesn't sound very patriotic."

"He's been saying the same sorts of things for a long time now, you know. And he gets things right, too. He said the Babylonians would come, and they did. Forty years ago he started saying they would come, and at the start, everyone laughed at him because no one could imagine Pharaoh letting Babylon run wild in his neck of the woods, but then Nebuchadnezzar came along and people stopped laughing. Then just a couple of years ago when the army of Pharaoh started to advance towards us, Nebuchadnezzar took his army away from our walls for a while. Everyone yelled and cheered and rejoiced, but Jeremiah said Nebuchadnezzar would come back with his army, and he was right again. And what about Irijah's grandfather, too? Look, if God says that Nebuchadnezzar is going to conquer Jerusalem, surely it's pretty stupid to keep fighting – but that's what your bosses want you to do. If they would just give in as Jeremiah says, lots more of you soldiers would stay alive."

It was a long speech. I don't normally talk very much, but sometimes things need to be said. Our leaders – even King Zedekiah – are all too concerned about their own skins and don't seem to care about anyone else's. Anyway, in this case the speech managed to convince Jehonathan's friends enough that they helped us lower the ropes down to Jeremiah. By that time, my eyes had got more used to the darkness and I could see that he was up to his waist in wet, slimy mud. At my insistence, he put some old clothes between his arms and the ropes – I had a suspicion that the mud would not want to let him go, and that we would have to pull pretty hard to lift him out. And so it proved. It wasn't thin, runny mud; nor was it thick, firm earth; it was mud into which you would pretty quickly sink, and then you'd be stuck there. We started to lift him, but soon realised that meant trying to lift all the mud out of the bottom of the cistern as well.

Lifting Jeremiah out of the cistern[41]

We pulled, and we pulled, but we weren't getting far, and it was clear that the ropes were cutting into Jeremiah quite badly. After a while, Jehonathan told Jeremiah to kick his legs around, and that did the trick. With various sucking and slurping noises, the mud finally let him go and

---

[41] Sweet Publishing/FreeBibleimages.org: http://freebibleimages.org/illustrations/jeremiah-cistern/ Slide 10

he was left dangling in mid-air with bits of mud falling off him.

When we got him up to floor level, he really looked a mess: covered with mud from head to foot and looking utterly exhausted. I'm not sure how much longer he would have lasted in that cistern if we hadn't come when we did. You wouldn't get much sleep if you were waist-deep in slimy mud that would drown you if you didn't keep your head up. And he was cold, too: he was shivering and shaking when we finally helped him up over the edge so that he could collapse on the floor.

Poor Jeremiah. We took him out of those gloomy depths and led him up to ground level where we helped to clean him up a bit. I insisted that he eat my lunch – there's precious little of any sort of food left in the city, so he wouldn't get anything otherwise. As the king had commanded us, we put Jeremiah into a room where he would feel safe and could recover from his ordeal.

You know, God expects a lot from his servants, particularly when it involves trying to warn others and save their lives. Yahweh cares, and he wants his worshippers to care too. I must admit though, I find it hard to care for people like Shephatiah, Gedaliah, Jucal and Pashhur.

So God did protect Jeremiah after all, but it's a bit funny that he should have done so through me – a foreigner, and a slave – when there are so many members of his chosen people who could have done the job. Maybe that is one of the reasons why Jerusalem is to be destroyed...

Part Two: New Testament

Twelve

No More Waiting

For the true story read Luke 2:22-35.

I wonder how soon I will die? God told me some time ago that I would not die until I had seen his Christ, and today, I saw him. So now I know that there is nothing stopping me dying, and I am amazed how much it has changed how I feel. Knowing that I wouldn't die until one special thing had happened has meant that I have never thought much about death, despite my age. Now I am thinking about death quite a lot, but I am filled with a peace and happiness which I could never have imagined.

What I saw was a complete surprise. Just imagine, if you can, seeing the great king as a baby – not much over a month old! Utterly helpless. Still not talking or walking. He doesn't even smile much yet, but he does look at you. I don't know if I was imagining it, but I don't think so – those eyes are something special.

A little baby – when I had expected a grown man, ready to be anointed and to rule as king. It's funny really, but I had just jumped to that conclusion, although God had never said it would be so. I still can't get over my silly misunderstanding, nor can I get used to the idea of a cute little baby as the Messiah! It makes me laugh to think about it. I'm a little disappointed though that it delays the time when he will be king. A little baby can't be a king. A little baby can't be a great prophet like Moses. A little baby can't lead his people to victory. So, for now, we'll all have to wait, and I suppose I will have to get used to the idea of dying soon, joining all of those others who are sleeping in the dust, waiting.

It started out as just an ordinary day in Jerusalem, and I had no plans to go to the temple at all. I got up early, as I always do, and prayed to God as usual. And that was when the day started to feel a little different.

During my prayer, I started to feel a sort of suppressed excitement, as if something wonderful was going to happen, but I couldn't think why. Of course, I have long had this hope that I would see the Messiah, and so he has always been in my prayers. Ever since God made me know that I would see the Messiah, I have tried to make sure that I prayed about this every day. Often, I have asked God for today to be the day, and sometimes I have asked several times per day. I had no good reason to think that the Messiah was more likely to be seen first on a feast day, but I have always felt that it seemed appropriate somehow, and so it was normally on feast days that I concentrated on my prayers for the coming of the Messiah. But this day was not a feast day. It was not a Sabbath. It was no special day at all, except for this feeling that it was special. So I prayed about the Messiah, but there was no lightning or thunder, no angel promising a day of miracles, just a thrill that went through me and left me even more excited than before.

My prayer was over and the day was just ambling along as any normal day does when I thought again about the Messiah, and suddenly the idea came into my mind that I should go to the temple to see... well, I wasn't quite sure what I might see, but I did know that I should go! Immediately.

Quickly, I made sure that I had everything I needed to visit the temple and set off. Not knowing how long I would need to stay for, I took an extra cloak with me as it was quite a cold day.

I was approaching the steps leading up into the temple when the strange things started to happen. My path had led me to a wider road, and as I joined it, I found myself beside a young couple who also seemed to be heading towards the temple. As an old man, they greeted me respectfully, and I saw that the young woman was carrying a sleeping baby, so I asked them whether they were going to the temple.

"Yes," the man replied, "it is the end of the time of purification after my wife gave birth."[42] He was carrying a basket which must have contained the birds for the offering: the offering of those who were too poor to afford a lamb.[43]

"Have you travelled far?" I asked.

"Not very far," he told me. "Just from Bethlehem."

---

[42] Leviticus 12:2-4
[43] Leviticus 12:6-8

"Bethlehem in the land of Judah," I responded quickly; "the city of David?" My heart started to beat a little faster, but I couldn't tell why.

"Yes, I am descended from David, so I had to be in Bethlehem for the census."

My heart continued its errant behaviour. Maybe this young man was the Messiah! Maybe that was the reason for my feeling of urgency in coming to the temple. How could I find out? I decided that openness was the best policy. "What is your name?"

"Joseph."

"Are you the Messiah?" I asked urgently.

He looked at me with wonder, then looked at his wife and smiled. Together they looked at me and together they said, "No." Again, they shared a smile.

"Oh," I said, disappointed. But then I began to wonder. Maybe this young man was the Messiah after all, but did not know it. "Are you sure that you could not be the Messiah?" I asked, doubtfully.

Once again, the look between the two of them before he answered, speaking the words very deliberately, "Yes. I am certain."

"How?"

By this time, we were walking slowly up the steps leading into the temple courts, and we were surrounded by quite a crowd of people. Now I was not the only one whose heart was beating faster, and my own heart seemed to jump a little with what I saw. The baby was stirring with the change in his mother's movements, and for the first time I looked at him a little more closely. He was not a particularly attractive looking baby, but there was no need to tell them that. So why was my heart pumping so hard? What was the cause of the excitement I felt? I found myself wondering what David had looked like as a child. Even a king starts life as a baby.

We reached the top of the steps and the vast courts of the temple were spread out before us, with the holiest buildings dominating the central area. Our temple is a place of exquisite beauty – fitting as a house of prayer for the living God. My companions were obviously not as familiar with the temple as I was, and were looking around uncertainly.

"Is there a place where Mary – my wife – could sit for a while to attend to the baby, and make sure that he is clean and ready to be presented before God?

"Yes, follow me," I said, and led them to one of the many walled areas that surround the temple courts within the vast colonnaded area. After that, I left them to themselves, pleased that presenting their baby to God was so important to them, but hoping that I would see them again to pursue an answer to my question.

I went to the gate which leads into the courts of the temple where only Jews can go and settled myself down to watch the crowds and wonder why God had moved me to come to his temple today. I thought about the couple and their little baby, and mused over Joseph's categoric statement that he was not the Messiah. How could he be so sure? The looks and smiles he had shared with his wife Mary had me puzzled. I could not divine the hidden meaning, and whichever way I twisted the problem it still remained insoluble.

After almost half an hour, I saw the couple approaching. The time had been used not only to prepare the child but also to prepare themselves, and the whole little family looked neat and tidy, happy together, eager to make the offerings to God. For a woman, the time after the birth of a child is an extended time of purifying during which she is forbidden from worshipping within the congregation and limited in many other ways. I wondered how long this couple had been married – their eagerness seemed more like that of a couple about to be married than one whose marriage had been blessed with offspring.

I think it was at that instant that the possibility first consciously entered my mind. Could this child be the Messiah? I was not even sure why the question occurred to me, but the excitement it inspired must have shown through, even in my old, bearded face. Before the couple could approach the gate to tell the priest what they had come for, I accosted Joseph.

"Is this child the Messiah?" I asked, breathlessly, and even as I asked, I knew the answer with the certainty that comes from God.

"Yes," he answered simply.

"Tell me how you know," I begged, and he told me the details: the visits from angels, the dreams, the visiting shepherds, the name given for the child, their early marriage.

"A virgin shall conceive and bear a son..." I murmured, suddenly seeing a connection I had never understood before, and it wasn't hard to imagine the difficulties that would arise from that situation! " 'Immanuel' – 'God with us'. 'Jesus' – 'God saves'."

I took the baby in my arms and praised God[44]

I quickly explained to Joseph and Mary what God had promised me: meeting the Messiah. This little boy was the fulfilment of so many of God's promises, including the one he had made to me. Gently I reached out and took the precious bundle from his mother's arms, then I spoke the words God stirred within me:

"Lord, now you are letting your servant
depart in peace, according to your word;
for my eyes have seen your salvation
that you have prepared in the presence of all peoples,
a light for revelation to the Gentiles,
and for glory to your people Israel."[45]

Joseph and Mary looked amazed at what I said – and very pleased. It was clear from what Joseph had said that they had found the visit of the shepherds helpful, and I expect that they will find that my story can help their faith too. Although I can't say that I know them well, their faith

---

[44] Sweet Publishing/FreeBibleimages.org:
http://freebibleimages.org/illustrations/simeon-anna/ Slide 4
[45] Luke 2:29-32

seems very strong – and they will need that strength. I am still struggling to understand just how important this child is. This must be the most important birth since creation! And God let me live to see it.

I said to Mary: "This child is appointed for the fall and rising of many in Israel, and for a sign that is opposed. Yes, a sword will pierce through your own soul also, so that the thoughts of many hearts may be revealed."

❧

How old must Jesus be before he can become king and bring about the consolation of Israel? No more Herods, no more Caesars, no more Roman armies dominating God's people.

How long, O Lord?

I must go and tell my neighbour about what happened today...

Thirteen

Follow Me!

There is very little specific information about Matthew the tax collector. For the real story, such as it is, see Matthew 9:9-17; Matthew 10:1-4; Mark 3:13-19; Luke 6:12-16; Acts 1:12-14.

If someone came to you one day and told you to follow him, would you do it?

I did.

But I had studied the person carefully before he chose me.

This was not just an ordinary person, this was the Christ, our coming king. At least, I wasn't quite sure of that at the time, but I am now. Our scriptures told of an anointed one who was coming, so he had to come some time.

Some time out of all the time in history had to be the right time.

And he came in *my* time.

And he lived in *my* town.

And he preached in *my* neighbourhood.

And his teaching made sense.

And then he said two simple words to me: "Follow me." So I did.

My wife thought I was crazy. My friends, the other tax collectors from all over Galilee, they thought I was mad too. Myself? Well, I thought it was an opportunity. An opportunity to get away from the love of money that had dragged me down into a spiritual dungeon. I had always loved the Hebrew scriptures: the law; the prophets; the Psalms. But life is busy, and married life makes more demands on one's time and money. And I always wanted to present a well-off face to the world too, I wanted to show people that I was above the poor people amongst whom I had grown up. I suppose it was simply a love of money more than God, really. It didn't start out that way, but Jesus is right when he says that money is deceptive. Originally, I was just seeking enough to live on, since even that isn't very easy in this corner of the Roman Empire. I worked hard doing any work I could get and we scrimped and tried to save, but actually ended up in debt.

And then I had this opportunity to become a tax collector. Now don't get me wrong, I knew that being a tax collector wasn't the best sort of job I could find, and I didn't really want to do it. I knew it wouldn't put me in a good position for winning a popularity contest, either! But it did promise enough money to live on, and even a little bit more, so that we could pay off all of our debts and maybe get ahead in the world. When I explain it that way, it sounds quite reasonable, but that just shows what my priorities were. Jesus says that if we look for the kingdom of heaven first, all the things we need will be given to us by our loving father in heaven. But I didn't trust that then. I do now, and so I know that it works – but back to my story.

The chief tax collector for the area was looking for more tax collectors. For various reasons, he had found this a surprisingly difficult task. Despite the stigma attached to being a tax collector, there were plenty of people who were willing to do the job, but mostly they were cheats and liars who would have sold their own mother into slavery if they could, and did their very best to cheat the chief tax collector and everyone else. People who would be more reliable were generally less willing to pay the social cost of being ostracised by their community for cooperating with the Romans. I'm not sure how he heard of me, but he came to visit me at a time when money was particularly tight. My wife had been sick and, of course, doctors aren't cheap. Our house needed work and the money I had borrowed to pay for the work was costing us a lot each month, just for the interest. And then, there was also the failure of the fish supply business that I had worked so hard to start. Debts, debts and more debts. It was a worrying time, really.

But then came the visit of the chief tax collector. The opportunity he offered was too good to refuse. I suppressed my twinges of conscience and signed the papers.

It was easy to justify what I had done. When my neighbours condemned me as a traitor, I replied that it was really their fault – after all, they hadn't been willing to pay my debts! What choice had they left me? Better me as a trustworthy collector, I argued, than most of the rest of the collectors, who cheated any way they could. Naturally, my neighbours weren't convinced, and after a while we moved to a different neighbourhood.

My wife was an orphan, and her brothers lived in other parts of the country – she felt that she had little to lose and that the comfort, fine clothes and jewellery would be a fair compensation. Maybe it was, for a while.

The income was good, and I paid off my debts and gradually started to accumulate money. My wife wore better clothes and we started to move in different circles. After a while, we moved to a larger house in a better area and things looked good for us – money always manages to look good.

But life had lost something. Our old friends didn't want to know us anymore. My parents were ashamed of me, although they tried to hide it. And I never seemed to find time to spend in prayer or meditating on God's laws. All too often, I couldn't even find the time to go to the synagogue.

Extra furniture, help around the house, fine clothes, special food and the friends that money buys so easily were all very well, but, of course, money needs more money to keep it company. A large house must be followed by a larger house. A servant needs other servants to supervise, and you can't wear the same fine clothes very often or your friends will start to think that you can't afford new ones.

Frequent parties, the obsequious attitude of servants and the admiration of our new friends all felt good, and the niggling of my conscience could be quieted when necessary.

But deep down inside I wasn't happy.

Money couldn't buy peace with God, and that's what I wanted most.

It was at that time that I heard of a new prophet called John who was baptising people in the Jordan River. I travelled to the place to watch and see what it was all about.

I saw many people baptised and met some of my fellow tax collectors there as well. Most of us were baptised by John, and then we asked him what we should do. His answer was simple: "Collect no more than you are authorised to do."[46] That was something definite to work on, so I did.

From that time on, I did not charge anyone more than a tax was meant to be. One of the common tricks of the trade was to take a man's goods if he didn't have enough cash and then put a low value on the goods. Sell them for a higher price, and the difference goes in your pocket. Simple and effective. But no more.

While I was watching John the Baptist, I saw another man being baptised. I noticed it because it started with a bit of an argument: John didn't want to baptise him. Ah, you might be thinking, he must have been too bad − but it was quite the opposite. John said he was too good and didn't need baptising. He certainly didn't say that about me! But this man convinced John to baptise him, and then an amazing thing happened; the spirit of God came down like a dove and rested on him. I saw it happen. And I heard a voice as well, saying that this was God's beloved son.[47]   That definitely convinced me that he was

---

[46] Luke 3:12-13

[47] Matthew 3:17

something special, and quite a few of us gathered around him and wanted to talk to him, but he was in a hurry to be gone. All I could find out about him was that his name was Jesus.

Jesus convincing John the Baptist[48]

I didn't see him again for a while, but then he moved to Capernaum and started teaching. The Pharisees seemed to hate him, mostly because he tried to help poor people, sinners, lepers and even tax collectors. I was still working as a tax collector, albeit a somewhat more ethical one at John's direction, and I knew they hated me too, so I thought that maybe I should go and listen to him. After all, peace with God wouldn't come if I kept doing the same things that had taken away my peace.

I went to listen and heard his teaching. I heard his words about what should come first in life, and I knew it didn't come first in my life. On other occasions, he taught about prayer, and I started trying to pray again. It was

---

[48] Sweet Publishing/FreeBibleimages.org:
http://freebibleimages.org/illustrations/gnpi-013-jesus-baptism/
Slide 3

frustrating but funny to notice how easy it was to get close to Jesus. Lots of people would press around him, until they saw me, the tax collector, coming! Then they sort of melted away and disappeared in the crowd, allowing me to walk up to Jesus and listen to what he was saying. He never turned me away. His looks at me were encouraging, but he never pulled his punches. "You cannot serve God and money,"[49] he told me once. Well, I wasn't the only one he was speaking too, but he looked at me when he said it, and the cap fitted.

I went and listened and spoke to Jesus on many occasions, and everything he said made sense, if you took the time to think about it. It fitted with the scriptures of old. Tax collecting got less of my attention and prayer got more. I made sure that I went to the synagogue every week and my wife started to ask questions about what I was doing. I told her a little of what I was feeling, and she said I should leave religion to the Pharisees, after all, they wouldn't welcome me in the synagogue, would they? It was true. They hadn't welcomed me. Not at all. Instead there was a deliberate turning of their backs to me and sneering remarks about collaborators and traitors. But it couldn't stop me. If Jesus went to the synagogue every week, shouldn't I too? I was becoming a disciple.

But there was still the blockage: money.

---

[49] Matthew 6:24

Jesus calls Matthew[50]

As I sat in my little booth one day, trying to catch up on paperwork, with papers strewn all over the table and coins in neat little piles, Jesus came and told me to follow him. Then he stood and waited for my answer.

By that time, I knew what I wanted to do, but... what about the money, the lists of people who had paid their taxes, the amounts that were to be paid tomorrow? Was it just the money that was speaking when I thought of how much trouble it would cause if I just left everything and didn't come back? If another tax collector took over my work, he would demand tax from many who had already paid. It wouldn't be fair. I looked at the money. Jesus had said that anyone who wouldn't renounce all that he had could not be his disciple.[51] I thought of the two bags of money that I had hidden in the wall of this very booth. Could I leave them? And it wouldn't stop there, as more words of Jesus came flooding into my mind: "Sell your

---

[50] Sweet Publishing/FreeBibleimages.org:
http://freebibleimages.org/illustrations/jesus-matthew/ Slide 3
[51] Luke 14:33

possessions and give to the needy."[52]   My wife was certainly not going to like this.   All that expensive furniture... but I couldn't really justify keeping it. After all, Jesus had left everything himself.

It took a bit of courage at the time, but I have never regretted it: I followed him.

PS: It was about two weeks later that I was able go back and tidy up the loose ends. I finished the bookwork to make sure that the list of people who had paid tax was complete and up to date. It seemed only fair. The money I left. My boss and my successor could decide what to do with it. I was free.

---

[52] Luke 12:33

Fourteen

The Wind and the Waves are Real

For the true story, see Matthew 14:13-32; Mark 6:30-53; Luke 9:10-17 and John 6:1-27.

When we left Jesus that evening, we were almost delirious with joy. Imagine feeding 5,000 men, plus women and children, and with just five loaves and two fish!

We had already seen water turned into wine, lepers cleansed, a dead girl raised to life and hundreds of other miracles, but the scale of this miracle almost defied belief. If we hadn't seen the whole process, and eaten the food ourselves, I doubt that any of us could have believed it. But we had tasted it, and I had even looked at the bread to see what it looked like. Each of the pieces I saw had the varying surfaces of dark and lighter browns that come from cooking on a griddle – a griddle that I knew these miraculous loaves had never touched!

And the fish too. Two small fish became enough to feed thousands. When Jesus does a miracle, he really does it thoroughly. Most of that fish we ate never swam in

Galilee, but I couldn't tell the difference between the parts that had and those which were the work of Jesus. As a fisherman, I'm rather used to looking at fish, and all the pieces seemed to have bones in the right places, and scales as well. We had often provided the fish for Jesus' meals and been very happy to do so. But now we had seen that he could make fish himself, which still amazes me. He certainly didn't need me to catch him any fish.

Anyway, we twelve got into the boat at Jesus' insistence. He would dismiss the crowd, he said, and he did too, though I'm not sure how. Even as we sailed away from the shore, the crowd that had refused to leave him alone all day were meekly walking away to their homes. That is true authority.

The delirious joy didn't last for very long, though, because the journey quickly became hard work. The wind was against us and the waves grew as darkness fell. We worked hard with sails and oars, but when the wind is against you, it can be quicker to walk.

That night, it was quicker. It was not long before dawn, but still completely dark when we suddenly saw something. The wind was strong and the waves it whipped up were making it difficult to use the oars very well. One moment your oar would be deep in the surging black water and the next you would be scattering a phosphorescent shower of spray as the boat rolled in the waves. We definitely didn't hear anything. The noise of wind and wave was much too great. We saw something – but what was it? At first we thought it might be another boat with its sails draped around the mast, but it was moving faster than we were and seemed much smaller than our own boat.

In the inky blackness of a stormy night on Galilee, while the wind-whipped waves continued to obscure any view we might have had on a calm night, it didn't take long before someone hit on an explanation: "It's a ghost!"

Alright, it was a silly suggestion, but it is amazing just how long your beliefs take to overcome your reactions. Knowing when you have time to think is one thing, but I still have some silly reactions when I don't take the time to think. I'm still ashamed of what I did with that sword when Jesus was arrested, giving the high priests the opportunity to criticise Jesus as leading a rebellion. My reactions learn slowly.

Anyway, we agreed it must be a ghost and were all shouting in fear, but as we did so, immediately the ghost spoke and then it wasn't a ghost at all. It was Jesus, and he told us to stop being afraid. Well, I wasn't so sure. Jesus had always come with us in the boat, hadn't he? I used to think it was one of the few things that he really needed us for, which was nice to know since he could do just about everything else. So I asked the ghost, "Lord, if it is you, tell me to come to you, walking on the water." It seemed like a good idea, at the time. However, like many of my good ideas, it seemed to come unstuck. Jesus said, "Come." Just one word, called out over the wind and floating back to me in the pitch black. What now? Had I really heard that word? And was it proof that it was Jesus? What to do?

Well, really, what would you do? Of course, if you knew it was Jesus, you would do what he said, wouldn't you? But did I know?

Nobody else was looking all that eager to step out into the blackness, so it was up to me, and that was how I found certainty. For a moment, a few precious moments, my faith was warm within me and my doubts were driven out. I knew that voice, even heard faintly across the roiling water, above the whining wind of a storm at sea. Jesus had said, "Come." Climbing carefully down out of the boat, I found my footing on the heaving waves and started to walk. It took some concentration and for an instant I was worried that I might fall over, and wondered whether I might hurt myself on the water. And that's where it all went badly wrong. Hurt myself on the water? Ridiculous! It was much more likely that I would drown in it with this wind tearing at my clothes and the waves rearing up over my head. I looked around – too far from the boat to go back; too far from Jesus to lean on his strength.

Beginning to sink, Peter cried out "Lord, save me."[53]

I will never forget the terror that enveloped me then, nor the feeling of sinking. The water sort of gradually "broke" underneath me; melted somehow – a bit like my faith was melting away. I tried to just ignore it and keep walking, but that didn't help. Suddenly, all support was

---

[53] Sweet Publishing/FreeBibleimages.org: http://freebibleimages.org/illustrations/jesus-water/ Slide 9

gone and I was falling, falling freely down into the terrifying water that seemed to open its mouth to take me, and I shouted out into the darkness and wind, "Lord! Save me!"

I knew Jesus was too far away to reach me, but who else could I turn to? And Jesus was there. Immediately. His hand reached out and held me. It's hard to explain exactly, but somehow, he helped me to climb up out of the water again, and stand there with him. My clothes were still wet, and they tangled around my legs as we walked, carefully, back to the boat. But now the water had congealed again and would bear my weight. Please don't ask me to explain how this worked. Again, I had this fleeting feeling of having to walk carefully lest I trip or slip and hurt myself, but this time, with Jesus there, the disastrous failure of faith didn't follow. Held up by Jesus' faith, we walked back to the boat together and climbed in.

How do you fight a battle against doubt? How – when the doubts are so real and the faith is so fleeting and insubstantial? The wind-whipped spray torn from the tips of the heaving black seas had been slapping against my face. That was real. Standing on water? Walking on water? That was only a hope. And my hope was overridden by my experience of life.

I had found that in the heat of the moment, I could not stop my doubts. All the practical powers of my mind and body conspired to drag me down to what my experience told me was "real". One moment I had been walking on water, and the next doubt had triumphed. What had changed?

Faith is not hard to rebuild once you have time to think. I spent a lot of time thinking about faith over the next few days. As a result, when many of his followers left Jesus after his hard sayings about eating his body and drinking his blood,[54] and he asked us twelve if we would leave too, I was ready with an answer. "Lord, to whom shall we go? You have the words of eternal life, and we have believed, and have come to know, that you are the holy one of God."[55]

It was never hard to have faith in Jesus' power: he did miracles all the time. The real test of our faith in him was to believe that he was the son of God. My failure of faith on that dark, windswept night as the real wind and the real waves triumphed over my fragile confidence had helped me to see this more clearly, and to find a little more of the true faith.

And I also wondered – if I ever saw Jesus again across the water, would I walk to meet him?[56]

---

[54] John 6:60-66
[55] John 6:68-69
[56] See John 21:4-8

Fifteen

To Go or Not To Go?

For the true story see Matthew 19:16-29; Mark 10:17-30 and Luke 18:18-30.

Jesus is an amazing man and the best teacher I have ever met. But some of his expectations are completely unreasonable.

Just a few moments ago, I got home after visiting him with a serious question. You see, I have always wanted to be a righteous man, the sort of man who walks with God and deserves the reward of eternal life. However, I also know that I continue to fail in many ways and that I need to do better. So I went to Jesus to ask what I should do.

The conversation didn't get off to a good start. I asked a straightforward question: "Good Teacher, what must I do to inherit eternal life?" But Jesus never seems to answer questions as you might expect him to, and this was no exception. "Why do you call me good?" he asked me, and proceeded to remind me that the only one who is good is God. Now I suppose he is right, in a way, because we only get our knowledge of what is good from God, and he was reminding me of that too – look at scripture, it gives you the answers! But we do use "good" in a relative way too and Jesus is good compared with every other man I have ever met, hence my initial greeting. Nevertheless, Jesus didn't like it, so I just called him "Teacher" from then on.

I still think he is good – the best man I have ever met – but I got the point.

Anyway, he went on to tell me to keep all of the commandments, and listed a few of the ten commandments that we all know, and that I have paid particular attention to all of my life. I have been blessed with a comfortable life, and I have tried to use it to give glory to God by obedience. I am in quite a position of power in society despite being relatively young, and have always taken this as a responsibility given to me by God. I could not let him down by disobeying his commandments. It seemed obvious to me that Jesus must feel the same, or else he wouldn't behave how he does.

But he is also so good at answering questions and has such amazing wisdom that I felt he might be able to give me more hints about what else God would want from me. What could I do to guarantee that eternal life would be mine?

I love God's law and I think about it constantly. Jesus made it clear that this was a good way to act, and it is certainly what he does himself.

It seemed to me that it was a matter of "so far, so good." But was there any more to do? Keeping the commandments was fine, but I could think of the words of various prophets asking questions like "what does the Lord require of you?" How important were those questions and their answers? Were they essential for eternal life? I really wanted to know what to work on next, or whether it was just a matter of keeping going as I was.

So I said to Jesus, "All these I have kept from my youth."

Jesus looked at me, and his face was a mixture of joy and sadness, even before he replied.

"If you want to be perfect," said Jesus, and I nodded before he continued, "go, sell what you possess and give to the poor, and you will have treasure in heaven." Jesus paused a little and looked at me hard before finishing with, "And come, follow me."

It was like being hit with a log and it stopped me dead in my tracks.

Sell what I own? Give it to the poor? But if I do that, I won't have it anymore. And how can I keep living a godly lifestyle if I don't have any money? Lots of people depend on me for help and I give lots of money to the poor. I can't become one of those lazy good-for-nothings who relies on everybody else to look after them!

I was so disappointed. I had expected Jesus to give me the ultimate answer for salvation, but instead he gave me a clichéd and simplistic answer that glorified his own lifestyle.

I have always been grateful for my wealth and used it for good. Throughout history, God has always blessed righteous people like Abraham, David and many others with gold and silver and immense riches. I want to use my wealth in the same way as they did.

But Jesus demanded that I give it all up: give my wealth away to people who won't use it for God at all! How can that be a good answer? Surely God wants my money used for him?

I know that the time may come when I do need to leave it all behind as Lot and his family did, and I have always tried to make sure I could do that in such a situation. But now is not the time. There is no disaster to avoid, and no catastrophe to assist with for which my money is needed. Everyday life will continue, and Jesus was demanding that I throw it all away and become dependent on others.

Ridiculous.

And if I started to sell everything, how long would that take? I don't like to boast at all, but I am a very rich man and all of those properties and goods would take months to sell, if not years. Does Jesus really want me to concentrate on nothing but money for the next year or two?

I was sad as I walked away from Jesus[57]

---

[57] Sweet Publishing/FreeBibleimages.org:
http://freebibleimages.org/illustrations/jesus-rich-man/ Slide 5

I came home, walking slowly, fairly sure that Jesus' demands were unreasonable, but wanting to make sure that I was right. And I thought of all the passages in the Psalms and in the wisdom of Solomon, and the message there is clear: blessings from God come to the righteous. How can it make sense to give all of those blessings away? Surely that is going against God's plans for the world, isn't it?

It's not as if I think of the money as mine anyway. I use it for God's work. I use my money for doing good things that God would want done. No question about that.

As soon as I got home, I sat down and started to write down my thoughts. I am completely committed to loving God and keeping his laws – yes, and loving my neighbour too – but I don't think it is a good idea to go against God's work by throwing away all the blessings he has given me.

I really like Jesus' teachings and feel that he has so much to offer to help straighten out all the wicked people in this world – they need his teaching so much. And he agreed that my keeping the law was good, so we agree up to there. But selling everything I have and giving the money to people who will squander it?

If only I had never gone to ask. I just can't do what Jesus wants. Did he know I wouldn't be able to? Was that why he looked a little sad before he told me what I needed most?

It's alright for poor people like his disciples. They had nothing much to lose anyway.

But, I ask you, could you do it?

Would you?

Will you?

Sixteen

A Gift for God

For the true story, see Mark 12:41-44; Luke 21:1-4.

I wonder whether I will eat tonight?

My neighbours all think I'm a bit mad, and sometimes they even say I'm irresponsible in my dedication to God. They say that I worry my neighbours and relatives because they never quite know when I might make an offering to God that leaves me with nothing.

Well, now I have.

But I don't plan to worry anyone. I won't be asking for help and I certainly won't be trying to get food from anyone. It was my choice to give my gift to God, and I'm not going to let them criticise God because I gave him my last two coins.

It was time for me to pay my tithe, and those two coins were just what I calculated that I owed. So, I gave them to God with my love, just as he had given them to me in his love.

But of course, I know that I can never out-give God. My life, my happy childhood, my happiness with my husband, my ongoing life since he died – all these things come from God, and I cannot pay him back for anything whatever I do. All I have came from him anyway.

So, no telling my neighbours and no telling my relatives.

Sometimes it's hard to do what you want to do for God, not because of your own attitudes or feelings, but because of others. At various times, people have told me that I need to plan more for the future and that I am being inconsiderate if I don't. People have told me that I make others feel responsible for my poverty or uncomfortable living near someone who is so poor. Sometimes it almost makes me feel guilty for giving to God, but I always tell them not to worry because God looks after me – they don't need to get upset. It's true, but they never listen. They keep worrying and some keep criticising, while a few actually do try to help – but they are rarely the ones who criticise.

A woman once told me that if people ever give me money, they will already have paid the tithe on it themselves, so there is no need for me to do so. Well, what would you think about that? It seems wildly wrong to me. I give at least a tenth of what I get, whether it comes from someone giving it to me or is part of the small amount of money I get from making and repairing clothes. I've never been rich, but I've never starved to death either – though that has never been thanks to the people who complain about my giving!

Anyway, I don't know whether or not I will eat tonight, but I'm very confident that I will not starve to death. When I die, it won't be of hunger, I know that. I have had this certainty for many years, based on the words of King David:

> "I have been young, and now am old,
> yet I have not seen the righteous forsaken
> or his children begging for bread.
> He is ever lending generously,
> and his children become a blessing."[58]

My father was a righteous man. He taught me the faith in God that I have treasured all my life, and I have never begged. I have tried to be righteous myself, although I can never be as good as I would like to be, or lend as generously as I would like either, nor am I as much of a blessing to others as I would like to be. Sadly, I let God down in these ways, but he never lets me down – so I know that when I die, it won't be of hunger.

God always gives and that's why I have to also. On quite a few occasions, I have helped people who had more than me. That annoyed my neighbours too, but really, they were people who genuinely felt that they had nothing and were worried about it. I knew that even if I gave them all I had, God would still provide. He always has. I don't know quite how he does it, but he always does: sometimes food lasts for longer than it should, sometimes merchants suddenly have to leave their stalls and sell off their items cheaply – just as I walk up. These things I have noticed, but I am sure there are many others that I don't even notice. I just can't possibly tell you how amazingly God works if you only let him.

---

[58] Psalm 37:25-26

People say that I am poor, but when I see the worry on their faces, the insecurity and unhappiness – when I see how much they desperately strive to make sure that they can provide for everything by themselves – I know that I am the one who is rich.

Poverty? How do you judge poverty? If you judge it by money, then I live in poverty, and the Pharisees and Sadducees are rich. If you judge it by contentment, then I am rich and they live in utter poverty.

They worry about fortune, fame, important positions and being treated with respect. On the other hand, I am completely content with a God who loves me and always gives me what I need. I have tried to explain and give them what I have, but they don't know how to take it. All they see is poverty, not the contentment and confidence that have come with it. If only they could realise that what I have is a blessing from God that makes me rich beyond their dreams! But who would listen to a poor woman when their measure of the value of a person is how much money they have?

How would they react if they knew that I feel sorry for them? It makes me giggle a little sometimes, but it also makes me thankful that I never had to make the decision to be poor. Maybe if I'd had to make the choice, I couldn't have done it any more than they can. Maybe money would have been my master as it is theirs. How much I would have lost!

She gave all she had[59]

This morning I ate the last of the food I had in my house, then I went to the temple to give those two little coins to God. It is such a blessing to be able to give back some of what he gives me. It is a bit disappointing that I cannot give the large gifts that some give, but at least I can give something and not have to go to worship God empty-handed. That would make me feel so ungrateful. My coins made a gentle jingle as they fell onto the huge pile of other coins in the box; I hope they can be used to give glory to our God. He deserves so much more than I can give, and I certainly don't deserve all that he gives me.

There, it happened.

As I was putting down my pen before, a voice called from outside my door. I opened the door and saw a well-

---

[59] Sweet Publishing/FreeBibleimages.org:
http://freebibleimages.org/illustrations/widow-mite/ Slide 3

off looking man. I have no idea who he was, but he said to me, "I believe you might need this."

He handed me a large basket with a cloth over the top. I must have looked puzzled, because he said, a little awkwardly, "Jesus said that you had put everything you had into the temple treasury, so I thought you might need this. I got some food from the market, and there's a little goat's milk in there too. May the Lord bless you and keep you."

Now that I knew what was in it, I noticed how heavy the basket was and pulled back the cloth to see what God had provided. Bread, vegetables, some grapes and even some dried figs! "You are too kind, my lord," I said. "I'm sorry, but I must take the basket inside; it is so heavy I can't keep holding it. Please come in so that I can prepare some food for you."

I ducked into the house and put the basket down hurriedly, then returned to the door. The man had gone.

So now I have all this food – so much food that even half of it would last me at least two weeks. What an opportunity: just down the lane I know a young widow who has a child, but no easy way of getting food. I must go and see if she has enough at the moment. She has been looking rather thin lately. What a blessing this is!

And then I must go and see if anyone can tell me who this man Jesus is. How did he know what I needed?

Seventeen

I'm Glad it was Dark!

For the true story, read Mark 14:12-52.

Just recently, I have been putting the finishing touches to a detailed account of the life of Jesus, based in part on my own limited experience, chiefly around his last Passover, but also on the much greater knowledge of various followers of Jesus who saw so much more of him than I did, particularly Peter.[60]

A lot of things can change in forty years. And as I look back over my life, I'm glad that's true. At the same time, some things don't change, even after 40 years. And I'm glad about that too.

That may sound a bit like a riddle, but I'll try to explain what I mean. When I was young – about 14 years

---

[60] 1 Peter 5:13 suggests that by the time Peter wrote the letter, a close relationship existed between him and John Mark, believed to be the writer of the gospel of Mark.

old – I heard of Jesus and I immediately wanted to know more. That hasn't ever changed!

And then, a couple of years later, I got involved in some undercover operations, trying to make sure that the chief priests and Pharisees couldn't attack Jesus, but it didn't work. I was young, and not very wise. I hope that that has changed.

By the time of Jesus' last Passover in Jerusalem, I was 16 years old. And my mother Mary[61] was a follower of Jesus. We had a house in Jerusalem, three stories high, with a large room on the second storey and sleeping chambers on the third floor. My mother had heard that Jesus wanted to keep the Passover in Jerusalem, so she had immediately spoken to my father to see whether our upper room would be available.[62] And my father agreed that Jesus could use the room. You might think that everything was settled then, but no, there was also a need to keep Jesus' movements quiet. The leading Jews were wanting to kill him, so it was best to spend the evening in a place that wouldn't be known to the Pharisees or high priests. And our place fitted the bill exactly.

But how could we keep it secret when his disciples didn't know the place either? That was where the "undercover operations" came in. And I was the one to carry them out.

Because of my mother's belief in Jesus and my own interest, I knew some of the disciples by sight, and my

---

[61] Acts 12:12

[62] There is no proof that the "large upper room" in the gospels belonged to John Mark's family, but in Acts 12:12, Peter went to this house and found many gathered there praying.

mother arranged for me to meet them and lead them to the house. Now, I was afraid that they wouldn't recognise me and that it would draw attention to us all if I had to go up and talk to them, so we arranged a special signal. And when it was all arranged it seemed very clever to me – and exciting.

I was to go to the place to meet them carrying a clay jar of water. And since that was normally a woman's work,[63] I would be easily recognisable by the disciples and they could follow me without us needing to speak at all.

A man carrying a water jar[64]

It worked, and Peter and John immediately followed me quietly back to our house and up to the upper room.[65]

So far, so good.

---

[63] No proof, but supporting examples: Genesis 24:14-15; John 4:7, 15; and a probable example of demeaning the deceptive Gibeonites by giving them "women's work" in Joshua 9:16-23.

[64] Sweet Publishing/FreeBibleimages.org:
http://freebibleimages.org/illustrations/last-supper-jesus/ Slide 2

[65] Mark 14:12-16; Luke 22:10-13

I'm Glad it was Dark!

It was evening when Jesus came with the rest of the twelve. I was watching out of a window, and saw them arrive and troop upstairs. I couldn't think of a good enough excuse through the evening to go into the room, but I kept watching and listening for any opportunity that might arise. And I saw Judas leave. Of course, now we all know why he left, but at the time I could only wonder.

After that, my mother began insisting that I get ready for bed, so I was bathing when I heard singing from the upper room, followed immediately by the sound of many feet descending the stairs leading to the street. And there was I with no clothes on. I desperately wanted to see where Jesus and his disciples were going, and here came my second bit of "undercover work". I quickly dried myself a little, slipped on my sandals and urgently wrapped a linen cloth around myself to be decent. And then I slipped out into the night. Just in time, too: the last few of them were just disappearing around the corner at the end of our street, and I had to run. As I reached the corner I could see them up ahead, and from then on I followed at a more leisurely pace, trying to keep them in sight, but myself out of sight.

Out of the city gates and down into the valley they went, seeming surprisingly subdued. I followed them across the Kidron and up the Mount of Olives until we came to Gethsemane, by which time I was starting to feel a bit cool in my hastily seized makeshift clothing. Early spring can be cold in and around Jerusalem. And it was clear that this night was going to be cold.[66] They entered the garden, but I continued to walk along the path past the

---

[66] John 18:18

place so that if any of them happened to notice me, they would think I was just another casual traveller in the night, rather than an excited youth trying to follow them and watch their every move.

After walking a short distance further, I stepped off the track into the garden and made my way slowly and silently back towards the group. The full moon made startling contrasts between light and darkness under the trees and I tried to stay in the absolute blackness of the shadows. I restrained my urge to hurry and inched my way along, guided by the quiet sounds the group were making. By the time I arrived nearby, hiding behind the trunk and branches of a tree, they were all making themselves comfortable – prepared for quite a wait, by the look of things. The dappled light made it hard to know exactly how many were there, but their comments made it clear that Jesus was no longer with them. He had gone on further to pray. For once, I waited patiently and watched. And listened. Soon I discovered that Jesus had taken three of the disciples with him. At once, I knew I must try to find them, but where had they gone? I didn't want to trip over them while searching. So once again, I was patient and watched. A real victory, that was. The disciples had settled down to rest, but they kept looking beyond them, and after a while I became sure that Jesus and the other three must have gone that way.

Slowly I scanned the blackness in the direction they were looking, but could see nothing. If I wanted to know what Jesus was doing, I would have to risk the possibility of getting caught. Immediately I turned around, preparing to move as noiselessly as I could, but my very first step let me down: a stick cracked under my foot while the dry leaves around it rustled. And I froze, still hidden behind the tree.

"What's that?" asked one of the disciples, sharply.

"It's probably just some small animal," answered another. "Don't worry. You're too edgy, Simon. Just relax."

"It didn't sound like an animal," replied Simon. "I'm worried about the chief priests' men. In the past, I would have known how to deal with them!" He laughed a grim laugh – or so it seemed to me.

And I stayed frozen. For as long as I could stay unmoving, I stood completely still. One of those men talking was Simon. And I had heard of Simon the Zealot. There were terrible tales about the Zealots; tales of cloaks and daggers, and sudden, silent violence. So I didn't move at all for a long time, and when I did, it was only to try to find a way to sit down without making any noise.

As it happened, the stick I had trodden on was about the only one nearby and there were actually very few leaves around, so it was quite easy to sit down silently. And so I sat, too afraid to try to find Jesus, and too afraid to return to the city in case Simon the ex-Zealot forgot his calling by Jesus. I got to know Simon later, and was never afraid of that most gentle of men again – but that was later. As I sat huddled against the tree, the immediate fear of a knife in the dark made breathing difficult. And so, time passed and I gradually relaxed.

All of a sudden, I woke to the sound of a scream, instantly drowned by shouts, and then Jesus' voice, loud and clear: "Put your sword away!" There were flickering lights amongst the dark shadows of the garden, and the shouts were suddenly silenced, replaced by a collective gasp. I learned later that this was when Jesus re-attached the ear of Malchus which Peter had cut off. But at the time, I was too befuddled by my sudden waking, and sleep still slowed my thoughts to a crawl.

Shortly afterwards, while I still sat leaning against the tree, there was a sudden rush, and several men ran past my tree and stumbled off into the darkness, running where no-one pursued.

And I finally began to wake up properly, so that when the noise of the crowd began to diminish, I stood up and peered around the side of the tree. A large crowd, with Jesus in the middle, was moving away from me, back toward the path that led down to the Kidron. On impulse, I stepped out from behind the tree and began to follow. And as I followed, I found to my consternation that four guards had been left behind, probably to make sure that Jesus' disciples didn't regroup and try to rescue him.

Two of them grabbed me, and if I had been wearing ordinary clothes, they would have caught me. As it was, I was able to yank myself free and they were left holding my linen cloth, while I ran away naked in the dark.[67]

I'm glad it was dark! In the darkness, I was able to get back into the city without too much trouble, but what would have happened if it had been light?

---

[67] Mark 14:51-52

Eighteen

He Promised us Life

Author's note: One evening, our family was having a meal together. I can't remember how it started, but somehow we ended up talking about writing stories and I mentioned that I was writing a story about Judas.

One of my daughters asked me, "Why would you write that, Dad?" and suggested that I could better spend my time thinking about the things listed in Philippians 4:8 instead of trying to look inside the mind of a traitor. I answered that I thought it was worthwhile trying to understand how a dedicated follower of Jesus could go so badly wrong – it might help me to avoid the same sort of failure.

What do you think?

For the true story, you need to pick through various parts of the four gospels and the Acts of the Apostles, particularly the passages listed below.

Matthew 10; Mark 3:13-19; Luke 6:12-16;

John 6:70-71;

John 12:1-7;

Matthew 26:6-16; Mark 14:3-11; Luke 22:3-6;

Matthew 26:20-25; Mark 14:17-21; Luke 22:21-23; John 13:2, 11, 26-30;

Matthew 26:45-50; Mark 14:41-46; Luke 22:47-48; John 18:1-6;

Matthew 27:3-8; Acts 1:16-20, 24-25.

What Judas did in betraying Jesus was terrible, and the reasons why he did it are not completely clear. — the Bible rarely discusses the motives of individuals. As a disciple of Jesus, he must have given up much, but at some time, he became a thief (John 12:6) and a traitor. At the last supper, Jesus said that it would have been better for Judas if he had never been born (Matthew 26:24). This story is just one suggestion of how Judas might have started going wrong, written with the intention of prompting us to be careful not to take steps that may lead us away from Jesus. Big things often start from small beginnings.

Paul said, "let anyone who thinks that he stands take heed lest he fall."[68] Let's take his warning seriously.

---

[68] 1 Corinthians 10:12

The note:

I'm about to kill myself. The rope is fast to a tree; a noose around my neck. A brief manuscript is attached to this note. I wanted to explain what happened; what went wrong, and why.

Someone's coming. No time.

What went wrong

My name is Judas, the son of Simon Iscariot. I was a godly man of letters. I was never a genius, but nor was I a fool. Jesus came into my life when I was looking; looking for something better than the endless striving for fame and fortune that seemed so pointless and destined to fail. If you are born into money, success is assured; for the rest of us, nothing is ever certain except hard work.

Jesus called me because – well, he never told me exactly why he called me, but I always thought it was because I could add a little more intellectual capacity to the group, and a little more knowledge too. I was not quite like the others, with their earthy, unsophisticated faith. Not for me the back-breaking physical work of gnarled hands and dangerous exertion. Refinement and an appreciation of cerebral pursuits were my bent – and possibly my weakness. Comfort was important, I admit it, but I always tried to control that desire within me. Certainly it was not comfort that Jesus called me to, yet I was happy to follow him wherever he led.

Truth to tell, I was rather pleased that he had chosen me above many others to be one of his special twelve. Only twelve out of all the men in Israel – and I was one. Twelve disciples; twelve tribes: twelve rulers to sit on twelve thrones.

Peter and Andrew, James and John – they were the foundation of the corps, and they were fishermen; not very polished in their presentation or accent, but rough diamonds in their own way. Peter was impetuous – he made me cringe on many occasions with his words, uttered so quickly without careful thought. Andrew was a giver: he was only ever a leader if he could only help others by leading. A wonderful servant of all – it wasn't hard to appreciate that characteristic. James and John were sons of thunder indeed, as Jesus' pet name for them suggested. Right is right and wrong is wrong, but Jesus was more for live and let live, and I agreed. James and John always seemed to want the destructive miracles from the scriptures of old, rather than the more constructive miracles Jesus practised. At times, it was difficult to keep them on the same path as Jesus, but I was able to help calm them down on several occasions before they led us all into trouble. Jesus seemed to appreciate that help – maybe that was what he chose me for.

A zealot – even a reformed zealot – is a difficult player to have on a team. I wondered why Jesus chose him, too. There was no doubting his enthusiasm or his genuine love for the law of God, but a zealot is a zealot, after all. Knives in cloaks were their style and Jesus was never like that. So why? I was grudgingly forced to admit that he seemed to fit in well with the group, and he certainly helped when there were questions as to whether God's message was really as serious as Jesus suggested. Simon had no doubts and argued his point very strongly – he championed the cause of law and argued that following God was the only important thing in life. I think he went a little too far at times, but he was a great help in showing just how serious godliness is in life.

The others were all an amazing mix too. Common, unrefined, uneducated and unsophisticated; but marvellously genuine, determined and faithful men. There were some with a bit more education and influence, though, like Matthew; and around him is built the story that led me to my doom.

Matthew had been a tax collector. He was used to handling money. Large amounts of money. I knew him before he became a follower of Jesus and used to envy him his easy lifestyle and his favour with the Romans which could smooth many of the waves on life's uneven sea. Back then, Matthew lived in a nice house with a nice wife and had lots of friends. True, they were mostly people like himself, but the uppishness of the religious Jews and their lofty disdain for his dealings with the Romans didn't affect his comfortable lifestyle much. But Matthew always seemed a little ill at ease with his life at that time; uncomfortable with the company he kept and unsure about how God would view him. Then he heard of Jesus and started to pick up his teachings, and appeared to become even more uncomfortable with his life. When Jesus went to him and called him, he made up his mind at once and grabbed the opportunity as if it were a bigger bag of gold than he had ever seen before. It was an incredibly courageous choice that he made that day, and he never looked back. I almost felt jealous of him when I saw his certainty.

But I, I had never dabbled with the Romans, never wandered from my clear understanding of the wonder of God's holy law and the obvious benefits that following it conveyed, both spiritual and intellectual. Matthew was repentant, but surely it was better never to have had such a blemish on one's record? I had kept myself from such sin.

We were quite a large group and needed someone to look after the money bag to make sure that it was kept safe and the money was all spent as it should be. For some reason, Matthew had announced that he didn't want the job at all. Out of all the rest, I was given the job – an important position of trust and responsibility. Nobody argued that I was the wrong man for the job.

A money bag[69]

I didn't know it then, but that was the beginning of the end for me. At first, the work seemed a difficult but worthwhile task. People would listen to Jesus' preaching and answer his call to seek first the kingdom of God.[70] Jesus spoke about the choice between serving money and serving God,[71] and said that no-one could be his disciple unless they were willing to sell or renounce all of their goods.[72] Of course, all of us twelve had already left everything we had to follow Jesus,[73] so we knew we had that part under control, but lots of his other followers were rich and tended to feel a bit guilty when they looked at us.

Not many people realised this, but looking after the money for Jesus was a big job. If Jesus had been a different sort of person, he could have easily been rich just from his preaching. But Jesus wasn't like that – and nor was I, at the start. People gave so much money that it was amazing. Obviously, a lot of people had a lot more money that I had

---

[69] "money bag" by rg1024:
https://openclipart.org/detail/31207/money-bag
[70] Matthew 6:33
[71] Matthew 6:24
[72] Luke 12:33-34; 14:33
[73] Matthew 19:27; Mark 10:28

ever had! And I had to arrange to dispose of it all. Poor people everywhere got to know me as their benefactor. Widows and their fatherless children welcomed me into their homes and looked to me for sustenance. It was a wonderful feeling. I knew that God's law was being satisfied, and there was even the feeling that I was helping the givers a little, taking away a temptation that could lead them away from the kingdom of God.

What I didn't learn soon enough was that any grand gesture we make, any big step we take towards godliness, any temptation we overcome – none of them end there. Grand gestures can often be cancelled, steps towards godliness have to be taken every day, and temptation always returns.

I had left my home; given up the little money I had; left everything to follow Jesus. But now I had the opportunity to get something back – easily and invisibly. The money bag was mine, and once everyone was sure that I was doing the job reliably, nobody ever checked on me. Nobody.

As a man who kept the law in all things, I fought this temptation when it first came to me, just as a passing thought, pushed away immediately. But then there was the day when I visited the home of an old man, very poor and all alone in the world. Giving some money to him was my last job of the day, and I was looking forward to going back to the others and having a rest. No-one answered the door and it took some time to find anyone who knew the man, but finally I found out the bad news: he had died just two days before and been buried immediately. Since the money would be no use to him anymore, I kept it.

Looking back, it is easy to see just how I failed the test that day. My policy was that all of the money earmarked for the poor should be distributed on the day it was received – I always knew that we might be betrayed to the chief priests or the Romans at any time, and I didn't want them to get any extra money if they did catch us. If somebody had asked me about it then, I probably would have stepped back from the precipice, but they didn't.

And from there on, it was all downhill to the end.

I built a wall in my mind – a wall that I never looked over and never asked questions about. On one side of the wall, I was Jesus' faithful disciple. On the other side of the wall, I started to collect money for myself. The other disciples didn't ask and were really rather naive about it all. Surely someone must have realised that a bottomless, uncounted bag of money could be a temptation?

Over time, I collected money and hid it carefully. But money without anything to use it for is not very satisfying. I had no "need" of money at all – as Jesus' disciples, people always looked after us and we were never short of anything we needed. Even when Jesus sent us out in pairs, Simon and I never had any shortage. One way and another everything just worked – but I'm mixing up the order in this story, because that was before I started collecting a little on the side. Anyway, the point is that money sitting in a jar doesn't give much satisfaction, and I started to see things I could use the money for. It had to be done carefully, because the only time I had a chance to use it was when I was meant to be going out and helping the poor. And not only that, but I had to keep helping the poor anyway or the truth would be sure to come out. But a small percentage could go missing and nobody would ever notice – not even Jesus, as far as I could tell.

That was one of the things that made me begin to question Jesus and his power.

I had always admired Jesus, admired his honesty and godliness and his astonishing ability to explain exactly what was meant by any passage of scripture. His miracles, too, were things that no-one else could do. He and I had spent many hours together, mostly as part of a group, but at times just talking by ourselves, and I had really felt that he was my friend. Jesus had a way of looking at you that was a bit different from anyone else. When you were alone with him, you had his complete attention and he made you feel special. If you said something to him, with a little bit of extra meaning left unsaid, he always understood, and I always felt that he was not a person I would like to try to keep secrets from.

For one thing, Jesus often seemed to know details about people when we couldn't see how he could have found them out. There was the time when the collectors of the temple tax asked Peter whether Jesus paid the tax or not. The teacher wasn't with Peter at the time, but shortly afterwards he talked to Peter about it. How did he know? I don't know how he knew those things, but it seemed very clear that he didn't know about my appropriation of funds, because he never said a word about it.

When I first began to take some of the money from the bag for my own needs, I began to avoid Jesus a little, just in case we ended up alone and he saw through me. But the problem didn't arise and gradually I forgot my worries – which fed my doubts instead. By that time, I had found a use for the extra money in a little gaming. There are always people around who are eager to spend some time with dice, and they are often eager to keep it all secret. Naturally, I was very careful: only ever at night, and only when we were in a city. I wasn't an irresponsible gambler, but at times I lost, and the debts had to be paid.

And Jesus never knew. That strengthened my doubts a lot, but I couldn't tell anyone. If the teacher was really the Messiah, he wasn't following the path we had all been taught. Helping the poor and healing the sick were not the hallmarks of the Messiah that we had learned about at school. Jesus did lots of teaching, but there were none of the victories against the Romans that a leader like Joshua or King David would have given us. And I began to see that it was all a bit of a farce. Don't get me wrong, Jesus was an amazing man and I had been happy to throw in my lot with him, but I felt maybe I had learned all I could from him. He was an amazing giver and teacher, but he just wasn't up to political leadership. I turned over options in my mind endlessly. Could we convince him to build up a force of godly, loyal men who could overturn the Romans using his miraculous powers? Simon still had many friends among the zealots, and many of them would leap at an opportunity to strike at the Romans with a better chance of wider success than their normal cloak and dagger actions. Could we convince him to take on the chief priests and highlight their corruption more, encouraging the ordinary people to join a rebellion? But as I had walked with Jesus, I had seen that whenever things started to get really big, heading in the right direction to appoint him king, Jesus seemed to work to keep things under control, as if he was afraid of what would happen.

Maybe it would be best to cut ties with him completely. Leave him and the entire small-minded enterprise.

My mind had been in turmoil for several months by the time Jesus first openly criticised me. It was just six days before the Passover and we were all in Bethany where Jesus had raised Lazarus from the dead. The family was giving a feast to say thank you. Martha was serving, and for some reason, her sister Mary took it into her head to pour more than a cupful of very expensive perfume all over Jesus' feet. Now I ask you, what was the point of that? I could have sold that perfume for about a year's wages. Just think what the local poor people could have done with some of that money! Families fed, children clothed, leaking roofs fixed, doctors' fees paid, and so much else besides. Well, I just dropped a simple hint of what could have been done, and the teacher criticised me in front of everyone. He tore strips off me, telling me to "leave her alone" and supporting that terrible waste!

I swallowed my pride and carried on as if nothing had happened, but the scene kept repeating in my mind throughout the next few days.

Then, just two days before the Passover, it all happened again. We were in Bethany again, this time at Simon the leper's house, and another woman came in with some very expensive ointment in a beautiful alabaster flask. Before anyone realised what she was doing, she had broken open the flask and started to pour the perfume over Jesus' head! Another year's wages gone dribbling onto the floor; more families who would be left in poverty while children starved and shivered in the cold. It was becoming an epidemic of waste and I started to remonstrate with her, but the teacher told me off again. In public – again. "You can do good to the poor whenever you want," he said, and he looked at me pointedly.

Frankly, that did it. If he was going to leave his roots of helping the poor, then what was left? He kept refusing to be a real Messiah and stopping the crowd from making him king, and now he refused even to help the poor.

I bit my lip and stepped back. I was angry and felt that Jesus had humiliated me. Looking back, I was probably too sensitive, but I always have been and Jesus must have known that. As soon as I could do so without attracting attention, I left the room and walked back to Jerusalem. As I walked, the words that the teacher had said earlier in the day rang in my ears: "after two days the Passover is coming, and the Son of Man will be delivered up to be crucified." Already the city was becoming busier, with visitors coming for the Passover from places all over the world, and the streets were quite crowded as I made my way to the High Priest's palace. Palatial it certainly was, and it wasn't easy to get in until I mentioned that I was a disciple of Jesus. Apparently, just that morning, the chief priests had been discussing how they could arrest Jesus. They had largely given up the idea of being able to get him before the feast, but my appearance rekindled their hope and they were eager to welcome me in.

I don't know who will read this record, but whoever it is, I need to say that the chief priests were not the sort of friends I would ever choose. I find money too attractive myself, but my attachment to it is nothing compared with that of the chief priests. For them, money is the start and end of life, the blood in their veins and the air they breathe. I think that Jesus went a bit too far in his condemnation of money – after all, we do need money to live – but the chief priests go much too far in their embracing of it. Being in their company made me feel ashamed and so mixed up inside. But my anger was still carrying me on, and the money they were promising was a help too.

Betraying Jesus was always going to be an easy thing to arrange. Jesus always seemed to assume that everyone could be trusted, although there was a funny wrinkle with that the very next day which made me wonder a little. Still, I'm sure that the teacher didn't suspect anything at that time.

Thirty pieces of silver were given to me and I was to come and collect a group of people at a convenient time when I could lead them to Jesus when there was no massive crowd around him, hanging on his every word as they always did.

After leaving the chief priests, I went and visited some poor families that we all knew well so that I could report that part of my activities when I went back to join the others. That night, we slept on the Mount of Olives as we had been doing all that week, but I didn't sleep very well, although I was sure that I was doing the right thing.

The next day the teacher wanted to have an early Passover feast with us and I was wondering if this might be the opportunity to have Jesus arrested, but here was where the funny piece of secrecy happened. Jesus arranged a strangely secret meeting to show where the feast was to be, so I didn't know where it was until Jesus led us there to start the feast. Apart from that, it would have been an ideal opportunity, but it didn't matter in the end.

There was one other disconcerting event that happened early on as we ate. Jesus made a strange comment about being betrayed, which got my attention immediately, of course. Everybody else was looking terribly sad, so I put on my sad face, but by this time, I had made up my mind and it wasn't going to change. Too many little reasons, and Jesus' public criticism of me had been the last straw. The money sealed the deal. Three years of my life wasted! I was really quite bitter about it.

Anyway, one by one each of the other disciples asked if he was the one who would betray the teacher, and finally it was my turn. Jesus answered me with a simple, "You have said so," and the conversation continued. The moment had come and gone so quickly that I almost couldn't believe it. Did Jesus really know? Surely he couldn't have known – I must have misheard him. Anyway, shortly after that I left and went to get the supporters I needed from the chief priests, but I wasn't sure whether Jesus would still be in the upper room when we got there, so I told them there was no hurry and instead, a few hours later, led them to the familiar place on the Mount of Olives. Jesus was arrested easily enough and all of the other disciples ran away like cowards. Jesus even called me "Friend", so he can't have really known what was happening.

Back to Jerusalem in the dead of night for a secret trial. They didn't want me as a witness – maybe they were afraid I would show up their false witnesses, but they showed themselves up with the foolish stories they told.

Despite all that had gone wrong between us, I really did hope that Jesus would show them all up, demolish the charges and maybe even escape to start a serious rebellion.

But it didn't work out that way. Jesus was found guilty on some trumped-up charges and it was clear that the chief priests were going to harass the Roman governor Pilate until he agreed to execute Jesus.

Jesus had prophesied that he would be crucified[74] and it was only the Romans who could do that. And that fact was the end of the road for me. Jesus was right, despite all the things he seemed to be wrong about, including the fact that he didn't seem to notice my little problems with money. Jesus knew.

---

[74] Matthew 20:19

So what had gone wrong? Jesus had promised life, but here it was ending in death – for him, and also for me. I couldn't face having betrayed an innocent man, and the chief priests didn't want to help me sort out my problem. I went to see them in the temple, trying to convince them to leave Jesus alone, but all they could say was, "What is that to us?" Priests arranging false witnesses to kill an innocent man, and yet they couldn't work out what it should be to them? No wonder Jesus condemned them as hypocrites!

I threw the money back at them and turned away. I can still see the coins bouncing on the floor of the temple.

My commitment to God's law has been corrupted. My honesty has been lost. My integrity lies in tatters. I have betrayed the son of God, and his last few responses to me have all been critical. There is nowhere I can go. It would have been better if I had never been born.

A noose[75]

---

[75] "Hangman's Knot" by gilmijar:
https://openclipart.org/detail/211634/hangmans-knot

Nineteen

Here is your Mother

For the true story, see John 18 & 19. For more background information, see the other gospels: Matthew 26:30-27:61; Mark 14:26-15:47 and Luke 22:39-23:56.

It was a very long, cold night after that last Passover with Jesus. First there was the time in the garden, when Jesus begged us to watch with him, yet we let him down by sleeping. Then came the mob sent from the high priests and led by Judas Iscariot. Peter's courage was never in doubt, but it was undoubtedly best that his wild sword-slash went astray or Malchus would have lost more than his ear. I knew Malchus and quite a few others of the servants of Caiaphas, and Jesus' miracle in healing him there in the garden certainly put a hole in their casual dismissal of his powers.

After that, we all ran away and Jesus was led back towards Jerusalem. Whether wise or otherwise, Peter and I followed the crowd and watched them take Jesus into the grand house of Annas, the former high priest, while everything was being made ready for this special night trial at Caiaphas' house.

The night dragged on, full of brutality and lies as they conspired together to kill an innocent man. In the cold of early morning, Jesus was taken to Pilate, and the Jews did their best to present him as a rebel who must be killed – unless Pilate was part of the rebellion.

Pilate gave in and handed Jesus over to them to be crucified. Of course, this was all a bit symbolic, because only the Roman soldiers had the authority, expertise and equipment to carry out a crucifixion, and they led the party out to Golgotha. I watched Jesus take up his cross and couldn't really believe just how badly he had been beaten.

I still had no idea what was going to happen. Surely Jesus, the Messiah, could not be crucified? But he had spoken about suffering, and I had learned that Jesus' words could be plain and simple or they could have layers of complexity that only became obvious later. As the crowd moved off into the crowded lanes, I was too upset to follow immediately. It was some time before I arrived at that horrible place, Golgotha – the place of a skull – in time to see the Roman soldiers take off Jesus' clothes and crucify him. For them it was simply business, and once Jesus was on the cross, they thought of their perks. His outer clothes were no problem: being of little value, they were divided into four parts and each soldier received his share. But the tunic was different; it was seamless and made in such a way that tearing it would be difficult and guaranteed to make it come apart. One of the soldiers suggested a game of chance and produced some dice for the purpose. It seemed so callous at the time, dividing the clothing while its owner was still alive and watching, yet it became a powerful proof of the power of God as we came to recognise the connections with David's psalm of suffering.[76]

Shortly after this, a messenger from Pilate arrived bringing the signs to fasten on the three crosses. These signs are used to describe the crimes that have earned each criminal a place on a cross. They also act as warnings, so they are often written in several languages to make sure that everyone gets the message that crime doesn't pay.

The criminals on either side of Jesus were easy: "For robbery," and everyone who read the signs felt a little safer as they walked home, and perhaps even a little grateful to the Romans for providing greater safety on the roads of Israel.

But what could they put for Jesus? The Jews hadn't even been able to get two witnesses to agree on anything, as you might expect when false witnesses are collected in a hurry. Pilate had his own ideas though, and the Roman administrator who brought the newly painted sign directed his servants to nail it above Jesus' head. As the board was nailed on the cross, I was standing near the high priests and their associates who had come to gloat. The charge read, "This is Jesus of Nazareth, the King of the Jews." It was probably fortunate that Pilate wasn't there to hear their reactions, as they weren't complimentary, and he is not known for his patience with opposition. In no uncertain terms, they told Pilate's representative that the sign was wrong and should be taken down at once. The Roman replied calmly that if they had any objections,

---

[76] Psalm 22:16-18

they would need to take them up with Pilate, but that until he received any further instructions from Pilate, the sign would stay.

Jesus on the cross[77]

By this time, all of the people gathered around had read the sign, and many started mocking Jesus because of it. I couldn't stand it. The master I loved was being laughed at by people who were not fit to tie his sandals, and that familiar fury was building up in me again. I had to get away or I might do something Jesus would not like, so when the high priest and his retinue left to see Pilate and voice their complaints, I followed. Pilate was not willing to give them a private audience, so I was able to hear the entire exchange, which didn't take long anyway. The high priest complained and Pilate responded with those now-famous words, "What I have written, I have written."

---

[77] Sweet Publishing/FreeBibleimages.org:
http://freebibleimages.org/illustrations/jesus-crucified-dies/ Slide 5

When I returned to Golgotha, my anger had completely gone. All that was left was a fear of the present, a fear of the future, and a despair that seemed to keep growing deeper. If only there was something I could do – but the one we always relied on to do the right thing was there on a cross. As I approached, there were few spectators left near the crosses except the Roman soldiers on guard. There were some women there, and I recognised all of them as followers of Jesus, women who had provided loving care, not only for him, but for all of us. One of them was my aunt, Mary, Jesus' mother,[78] and I couldn't help feeling very sorry for her. As her nephew, I knew enough of her courage and faith to see that she could never have been anywhere else, but what a terrible, heart-wrenching circumstance it was. Her sister, my own mother Salome, was standing next to her with an arm around her, and I stood nearby in silence. I gazed at the soldiers lounging around at the foot of Jesus' cross, looked at the shadows cast by the sun, watched some birds flying in the morning sunshine – anything, in fact, to avoid looking at Jesus. But then Jesus called out to his mother, his voice strained, but controlled: "Dear woman, here is your son." Then he looked directly at me and said, "Here is your mother."

They were simple words, but Jesus had given me something to do. My own mother was there listening as Jesus gave me another mother to care for. It was a responsibility he could no longer undertake. But then it

---

[78] Various verses suggest the conclusion that Mary the mother of Jesus was the sister of Salome who was the wife of Zebedee and mother of John. Some are: Matthew 27:55-56, Mark 15:40-41 and John 19:25.

occurred to me: What about his brothers? They were there, somewhere in the city, present for the Passover feast as all Jewish males must be. But none of them was there at the cross of the real lamb of God.

Jesus' request made me think deeply. He obviously thought it better to entrust his mother to a nephew who believed in him, rather than leaving her with one of her sons who did not believe. It reminded me of his words that his family were those who did the will of God,[79] and now he was asking me – as a brother – to look after his mother in preference to James, Joseph, Simon and Judas, who were still waiting somewhere else for him to finish his work.

More than anything else that happened, this request showed me just how serious Jesus was when he talked about us as a family of believers. Unbelievers were not part of the family, and the family should look after its own. What a responsibility! And what a way of showing just how close our relationships within the fellowship of Jesus are meant to be.

Later, Jesus' brothers came to believe in him and became his servants,[80] joining Jesus' true family – the ones who, like him, serve his father in heaven.

---

[79] Matthew 12: 46-50; Mark 3:31-34; Luke 8:19-21

[80] James 1:1; Jude 1:1. The letters of James and Jude are believed to be written by Jesus' brothers James and Judas.

Twenty

A Vacant Place

For the true story, see Acts 1:15-26.

Jesus had gone into heaven from the Mount of Olives a few days before. We, his followers, were still waiting in Jerusalem for the gift he had promised us. Meeting together often in the upper room, we talked incessantly. Not meaningless, repetitive chatter or gossip, but useful, productive discussions, as faithful men and women strove together to understand the work of Jesus and their place in it. There were so many questions, and as each was asked and discussed, so many of the teachings of Jesus fell into place for us. Statements which had seemed obscure and awkwardly symbolic, now seemed crystal clear in the light of his death and resurrection. The upper room had become a place of warm fellowship and a new understanding.

Then Peter raised the vexed question of Judas and the thrones promised to Jesus' disciples. Twelve disciples. Twelve thrones. Twelve tribes. But only eleven disciples remained. Judas Iscariot had taken his own way and would never sit on a throne judging one of the tribes of Israel.

What should be done?

Judas had betrayed Jesus and led a crowd of religious officers and soldiers to take him prisoner. Once he saw that Jesus had been condemned, he thought better of it, but took the coward's way out – instead of trying to rectify his failure as Peter bravely did. Jesus had said that it would have been better for his betrayer if he had never been born, and Judas sought a noose instead of forgiveness.

There were many ghastly reports and rumours about what had happened to Judas, but as far as I can tell, after throwing the blood money down in the temple, he went to an unused plot of land and hanged himself by a rope from a tree. His body was found the following afternoon while Jesus was still on the cross, but with the Passover feast imminent, no-one was willing to make themselves unclean by taking down his dead body. The news was apparently passed on to the chief priests, and there the matter rested. After Jesus' resurrection, the chief priests weren't very eager to talk about the subject at all, so the body was left hanging while they secretly arranged the purchase of the unused plot, using the very money they had paid Judas for his betrayal of Jesus. The plot has since become a burial place for foreigners who die in the city while on a pilgrimage. A field of death bought with blood money. Meanwhile, Judas' body remained hanging from the tree, slowly decaying. It seems that last week his neck finally parted and the body fell to the ground and burst open, with all Judas' insides gushing out onto the ground. A sad end for a man who had had so many advantages and opportunities. I knew him well.

Nevertheless, his absence posed a difficult question: what should be done? Peter reminded us of some words of David in the Psalms: "may another take his office."[81] It made sense. Twelve judges would be needed to sit on the twelve thrones Jesus had said were already prepared.

It did not take long to agree on that, but the next step took quite a while. How would we choose the replacement?

Well, that was a very tough question. Finding candidates was not hard, although there were many opinions about that too. Hours of prayer and discussion were required to conclude that we should consider only people who had travelled with Jesus from the start of his ministry. After all, the twelve disciples had to know all the things Jesus had taught. It was acknowledged that there were some things which Jesus did only with the twelve, but then again, there were also some specific occasions where he took only three or four of the twelve for some special events. Someone who had stuck to Jesus from the start was the closest we could get to someone having the same background as the twelve.

Funnily enough, there were at least as many women who had done that as men, and someone even asked whether the replacement could be a woman. That was answered fairly quickly – Jesus had chosen men as his disciples, despite those same women being already such consistent followers. Others also pointed out that Abraham, Isaac and Jacob were all men, as were the fathers of the twelve tribes and all the kings, and that Eve had been made for Adam, not Adam for Eve. Still others

---

[81] Psalm 109:8

reminded us that, while Jesus had not excluded women from following him – and had often defended individual women from criticism, and even from stoning in one case – he still had not chosen them as leaders.

This was a tentative but wonderful time for Jesus' followers, as we learned to work together to find God's way when Jesus was not there to tell us. We didn't just pray and then make up our minds; nor did we talk and talk before finishing with a final prayer for blessing. Rather, we prayed frequently throughout. Whenever there were differences of opinion, we would stop and pray. It is amazing how much more clearly one can see God's way when prayer is a first port of call, not a last resort. Some complain that it takes too long, but I can't help thinking about Jesus spending entire nights in prayer struggling to determine what was best. It often wasn't easy for him to know what was best, and since that was his solution, I'm sure it should be ours too.

Many thousands of people had followed Jesus in the early days. Wherever he went, crowds were everywhere. While I'm certain he would have been very popular even without the miracles, the miracles guaranteed an eager following.

Jesus' most popular miracle was the feeding of 5,000 men, plus women and children. The next day, many wanted a repeat performance, but instead, Jesus made some of his most difficult statements ever: about eating his flesh and drinking his blood. Followers who had just come for a feed gave up and left immediately. Many of his long-time followers were so upset that they left too – so many, indeed, that Jesus even asked the twelve whether they would be leaving too. But they couldn't. Of course they couldn't. Jesus' words were life, and there was nothing better available anywhere. We just had to try to understand, not run away.

Anyway, the numbers built up again after that, but there were not many of the original followers left – just the twelve, a very few other men, and the women who always looked after Jesus so kindly. I think they all would have loved to mother him, and probably quite a few of the younger ones would have liked to marry him, but Jesus always remained a little aloof in some ways. His dealings with women were always infinitely kind, utterly friendly and helpful, but completely exemplary. Quite unique.

Many new followers joined the existing few, and stayed with the twelve through the dark days while Jesus was dead. Those were days when we didn't really know which way to turn. We thought of giving up. Those few days taught me a very important lesson about how blind I could be, failing to see the simple prophecies in scripture and spoken by Jesus. It made me realise that others will be like that too, and causes me to be much more patient when I teach people about Jesus.

So there we were. About 120 people with a wonderful hope and strong fellowship – and a very important task to do: replace Judas. We started by thinking out loud about those who had been with Jesus from the beginning; it was quite an enlightening experience. It made us understand why Jesus had said that many are called but few are chosen. Thomas might say, "Remember so-and-so?" and name an enthusiastic follower who had encouraged us greatly, until his father had died and his inheritance had claimed him. We would sit for a while and remember his useful contributions and feel sad that the love of the world had overcome his love of Jesus.

In the end, there were only two who had been with Jesus from the start when he was baptised by John, and were still with the believers that day.

Only two: Matthias and Justus.

But two was as bad as twenty. How should the choice be made? Everyone who spoke agreed that the two were faithful and committed followers of Jesus, but which would be better for this important job? One of the two pointed out that he had been available when Jesus had chosen the twelve and that Jesus had not chosen him, so he would only want to take the position if he could be sure that it was Jesus' will.

Everyone agreed with that too.

Someone mentioned a passage in Proverbs:

"The lot is cast into the lap,
but its every decision is from the Lord;"[82]

then suggested that we should draw lots to find which of the two would be the right one. Another agreed, and mentioned a second passage:

"The lot puts an end to quarrels
and decides between powerful contenders."[83]

That was certainly what we wanted. No quarrels, and a decision between the two who met the requirements.

After a while, everyone agreed, and we prayed for guidance through the lot. The lot was cast and Matthias

---

[82] Proverbs 16:33
[83] Proverbs 18:18

was chosen. He was accepted into the number of the twelve and will be among them when they sit on twelve thrones judging the twelve tribes of Israel.

Matthias joins the eleven[84]

Once again, I had not been chosen.

When Jesus had first chosen the twelve, I had felt judged and rejected – until Jesus had comforted me. There has never been a man with such compassion and empathy as he. He knew that I was worried about what was wrong with me.

---

[84] Sweet Publishing/FreeBibleimages.org:
http://freebibleimages.org/illustrations/jesus-ascension/ Slide 11

Jesus explains[85]

He reassured me that I was not being rejected as ungodly or a failure, but that this task was not the right one for me. He encouraged me to continue and never give up, so I did. I stayed with Jesus through times of both joy and worry, and felt that I had learned so much from him. At times, it had occurred to me to wonder whether possibly I would have been included if the twelve had been chosen later, once I had learned more from Jesus.

Now I knew the answer: I was still not the right person.

Jesus' words to me have always stayed with me, and they supported me during the time after Matthias was chosen. Despite the joy of Jesus' resurrection, they were difficult days for me. Rejection is hard to cope with, and a double rejection seemed almost unbearable. What confidence and faith could I have when I knew I did not make the grade? The other believers saw that it hurt, and they could understand why. It was one of the much newer believers, another man named Joseph, who started me

---

[85] Sweet Publishing/FreeBibleimages.org:
http://freebibleimages.org/illustrations/jesus-ascension/ Slide 2

thinking on the right path again. He reminded me that he had only met Jesus for the first time less than two months before he was crucified. For him, the wonderful discovery of an utterly reliable leader had been such a fleeting joy as his master had been snatched away and crucified. He had had very little opportunity to know Jesus and to learn from him, and he was envious of the years I had spent in the company of the saviour. It got me thinking again of Jesus' words that he had not rejected me; it was just not the right work for me.

With prayer and help from my brothers, I got over the hump and went back to the motto Jesus had given me, "Never give up!" Jesus did not want me as a leader – he wanted me as a servant, and how glad I was that he wanted me at all!

Matthias did his work well as one of the twelve, starting with a major test on the day of Pentecost just a week later, and a crown of righteousness is laid up for him.

I'm so glad I didn't let his acceptance by Jesus make me stumble and lose my faith in Jesus.

Never give up. Jesus knows what is best for you better than you do yourself.

Historical note

Joseph, also called Barsabbas and Justus, was probably the brother later sent with Paul and Silas to carry the letter from the elders after the conference in Jerusalem. At that time, he is called Judas Barsabbas (see Acts 18:22) and spoken of as one of the leading men among the brethren. In Colossians 4:11, Paul writes of one Jesus, called Justus, a Jew who was a fellow worker for the kingdom and who had been a comfort to Paul. Could this also be the same disciple? Some people in the Bible have several different names.

Twenty-One

The Ethiopian Eunuch

For the true story, see Acts 8:26-39 with references back to the visit of the Queen of Sheba in 1 Kings 10:1-13 and 2 Chronicles 9:1-9, and exclusion from the assembly of God in Deuteronomy 23:1. The prophecies of Isaiah that are referred to are from Isaiah 56:3-5 and Isaiah 53:7-8.

I just got back from an absolutely wonderful trip to Israel and I really want to tell you about it.

Almost three months it took, but it was well worth the time. Candace, the Queen, gave me permission to go – in fact, she was quite eager that I should go and visit Israel, as one of her predecessors had done almost a thousand years ago in the time of King Solomon. Some of the items of jewellery he gave as gifts at that time are still among the treasures I take care of for her majesty.

Travelling with a large group of officials and servants is always slow, and thirty days elapsed before we saw the walls of Jerusalem. Perched on a ridge among hills, a characteristic yellowy brown marks the city walls and also stains the ragged assortment of buildings that have overflowed those ancient boundaries.

Our accommodation had been arranged beforehand in the area where Romans and other foreigners live. The Jews do not like visitors to be too close – even visiting dignitaries.

Discussions and meetings filled much of the next two weeks. Senior Roman administrators and army officers entertained us hospitably, although the governor of Judea himself was busy in Caesarea and could not spare the time. Realistically, the mere treasurer of a queen of Ethiopia is not all that important anyway, but I knew she would not be pleased when I returned. I could picture her lips pursing tightly and her fingers drumming on the arm of her throne as I reported this – possibly I could gloss over it with other, more flattering details.

The chief priests of the Jews were quite eager to see me – I think money is always an attractive subject to them. The Queen had asked me to deliver some carefully chosen gifts and to make enquiries as to whether there were any cultural exchanges which could be arranged. Diplomatic discussions are mostly couched in fulsome terms, and almost-commitments are often made without any intention of ever bringing them to fruition. The chief priests were eager to accept the gifts, but not so eager to take any concrete steps towards an ongoing relationship with non-Jews. Nevertheless, it was a busy time, and I hope that my queen will be satisfied with the outcome. Written tokens of appreciation were given and received, and maybe some future benefits will accrue.

For me, those things were all necessary but tedious activities, and I was glad when they were over and I could concentrate on my real reason for coming to Jerusalem. Don't get me wrong, I do hope that my nation can forge closer ties with Israel, but the chief reason was the God of Israel. I made this long and difficult journey so that I could worship the God I want to claim as my own.

God's temple in Jerusalem is an enormous and truly beautiful edifice, skilfully formed in marble and gold. The worship he requires is even more beautiful – and demanding. The God of Israel is a living God, vastly different from the gods of my homeland, and it was his living work that attracted me. The gods my extended family worshipped were not the same. Too often they seemed to have been created by people with the characteristics of spoiled children. Inconsistent, trivial, arbitrary, greedy and utterly self-seeking, these gods did not impress me.   Constantly squabbling amongst themselves, the gods of my homeland, of Greece or Rome or any other nation, are, if anything, worse than the people who worship them. The God of Israel stands alone, not just head and shoulders above the others, but rather as the *only* living God, who walks over the useless images of these so-called gods.

☙

As a young lad, my father used to take me to the river Nile and we would sit quietly and feast our eyes on nature. My father was fascinated by birds, and he wanted me to be too. Sitting quietly in places where shrubbery and trees hid us from the birds, we could often observe them doing things that few would ever see. We saw their care for their young, watching them as, at times, they sat utterly, astonishingly still on a nest while people or animals walked within arm's reach of them, but without ever seeing them. Brightly coloured birds with plumage which shone in the sun, painted in stark contrast to the surrounding vegetation; these we saw, yet despite their brilliant markings, they were completely invisible so much of the time.

Yes, it was birds that convinced me that there had to be a creator who was greater than the wide range of gods worshipped in my country. I saw a creation which reflected a single controlling force. I did not see any evidence of a collection of "special-interest gods", said to be powerful in only one geographic area, or in one aspect of nature – and often portrayed as squabbling like delinquents with other equally petty minor deities. No, nature convinced me of the existence of a single god, one god who had created everything. Not only that, but, given the selfish and destructive nature of human beings, the creator must still be in control for life to continue as it does.

My father was an important official, called later in life to the court of the queen, and he found peace and comfort in the time he spent watching birds. In observing nature, he too had been led to a conviction that there must be a creator. Being well educated, he had heard the myths and legends about Solomon, and one of the common threads through all of the stories was his belief in one God. Only one. Of course, these stories were told with overtones of a cultural superiority which showed sympathy to Solomon for his lack of understanding of religious matters: "Poor old Solomon, wise beyond words, they say, but even he didn't know the gods as we know them – even our little children know more than he did."

My convictions were otherwise. Having watched the feathers of birds spreading out, wider and flatter until gossamer-thin as they slowed to land ever so softly on the wind-ruffled water, I had perceived God in his creation. I also saw him in the sudden lunge of a tern, judging to perfection the flittering movements of a hapless insect on the surface of the river – plucked up and swallowed in an instant, leaving never a splash to mark its passing. And this God I recognised in the words of the ancient scrolls, brought back from Israel by our queen so many centuries before. Lovingly kept, but rarely read by those who did not want to know him better. My father had read them, read them with love, and when his beloved birds convinced me too of the God of Israel, he contrived to give me the same opportunity.

King Solomon's scribes had been very busy during the queen's visit. The Book of the Law of Yahweh had been copied out in Hebrew and presented to the queen, but that was not all. Another scroll had been written in our language, translated by the expert scribes of Solomon, whose knowledge of languages was without parallel in the world. Over the years, new copies had been made by expert scribes, updated as necessary to reflect the changes in our language – our words and script have changed over the centuries as all languages do. However, the most recent copy now is still at least two hundred years old, and only a determined reader can discern its meaning. My father had led me through its lessons, and so the laws of the God of Israel had gained another disciple in far-off Ethiopia.

Reading a scroll[86]

❦

Worship was my goal in this visit to Jerusalem. The problem was that I was a eunuch. All men serving in the queen's palace are eunuchs. This has been the rule for many generations – they cause less trouble that way. My father was not called to the queen's service until after I was born, or else I would never have been born.

In the law of the God of Israel, I found that men who had been injured in the private parts could not enter the assembly of God. Did that include me? After studying the words used for quite a while – this was important to me – I decided that I couldn't be sure. It might. It might not. Greater expertise with the original language might help, and so my quest to visit Jerusalem began.

---

[86] Sweet Publishing/FreeBibleimages.org:
http://freebibleimages.org/illustrations/philip-ethiopian/ Slide 2

It had taken several years, but finally I was ready to set off for Jerusalem. I could hardly wait to see the temple of the God I worshipped, and I hoped beyond hope that I would be able to offer my worship within its courts.

CR

Obtaining an audience with an expert in the law was not difficult once the gifts and financial arrangements had been agreed, and early one morning I was ushered into the presence of Gamaliel, one of the most revered teachers in Israel. We met in a room near where we were staying. Notwithstanding my commitment to Yahweh, Gamaliel was obviously not willing to welcome me – a foreigner – into his home, or even visit me in my temporary home.

Now was the opportunity to get a definitive answer to my question: Could I enter the temple to worship? I explained the situation to him, and he looked doubtful as he smoothed his moustache. I explained that I had been circumcised, so that was not a problem. Gamaliel still looked doubtful and continued to smooth his moustache. Eventually, he found his voice and gave me the bad news, "No, I'm afraid you cannot enter the temple or the congregation," he said. "Your situation is highly unusual, but our scriptures must exclude you from worshipping in the temple. Moses' words are to be understood in this way."

That was it. No opportunity to argue, and no chance of appeal. If I wanted to worship, I must do so from outside the temple. For an instant, my temper prompted me to pack up immediately and leave, but that would have been foolish. The Creator-God I worshipped must still be worshipped even if he excluded me from formal worship with others. My worship must be offered outside the temple. Only my gifts would be able to find their way into that holy place.

❧

One other goal I had set myself. I wanted a scroll of the Jewish scriptures. The law and many Psalms and proverbs I could read in my own country, but I had heard of Jewish prophets who had spoken words from God and predicted the future, centuries before it happened. Money was no issue – my queen had made me a very rich man – but could I find someone who would be willing to sell me a scroll of the words of one of the great Jewish prophets? I read some of the available scrolls in Greek, and decided that a scroll of the prophecies of Isaiah, Jeremiah or Ezekiel would be best. I made enquiries and offers, and then I waited. Waiting for a week with no certainty of success was rather difficult, but finally, late one afternoon, I was introduced to a scribe who was willing to sell me a scroll of Isaiah for a large sum. Such a scroll represented about three months of work, but the fee demanded would have kept a scribe living in luxury for at least a year!

However, I jumped at the opportunity, paid the money, and gave extra gifts liberally to the scribe and the middle man who had brokered the deal. Victoriously, I carried the scroll away and went to my lodgings. Urgently, I removed the beautifully decorated outer cloth, with its Hebrew lettering and coloured embroidery. Quickly, but carefully, this was followed by the linen wrapping which kept at bay the enemy of all scrolls – moisture. In my hands I finally held my own copy of God's word through

Isaiah, and I was eager to read it. During the evening, I read the scroll from end to end. The beauty of many sections of the words struck me forcibly, and the repeated insistence on the sovereignty of God thrilled and satisfied me. One particular passage stood out above all others:

> "Let not the foreigner who has
> joined himself to the Lord say,
> 'The Lord will surely separate me from his people';
> and let not the eunuch say,
> 'Behold, I am a dry tree.'
> For thus says the Lord:
> 'To the eunuchs who keep my Sabbaths,
> who choose the things that please me
> and hold fast my covenant,
> I will give in my house and within my walls
> a monument and a name
> better than sons and daughters;
> I will give them an everlasting name
> that shall not be cut off.' "[87]

This was healing balm to the soul of a foreign eunuch who had just been refused entry to God's house. The passage continued with the heart-warming assurance that this house of the Lord was to be a house of prayer for all nations.

Some other parts I had merely read quickly and noted as difficult. Tomorrow, we would start our return journey, and I would be able to read the scroll several times during the trek.

---

[87] Isaiah 56:3-5

☙

Leaving Jerusalem was difficult. I had come to worship, and worship I had, but only by myself – the temple had remained closed to me. The religion of Israel had not accepted me, although the passage from Isaiah encouraged me to believe that the God of Israel had. I was leaving with the impression that the religion God had given to Israel was delightful and pure, although those who led it seemed to concentrate too much on appearances, and too little on actually being like God.

We took the desert road leading to Gaza, planning to join the coast road there and continue towards Egypt. Isaiah's scroll was on my lap almost before we had cleared the gate, and I was utterly absorbed as the chariot made its way over the packed earth road. My driver had instructions to minimise the roughness of our travel, as I did not want my prized possession to be damaged or lost through careless driving. I also intended to make notes as we travelled, and writing legibly in a moving vehicle is difficult.

All that day, I read and re-read. Some parts were marvellously simple to understand. Others had to be read several times before an elusive comprehension could be achieved. Towards the end of the day, just before we stopped at an inn for the night, I came across the passage:

> "Like a sheep he was led to the slaughter
> and like a lamb before its shearer is silent,
> so he opens not his mouth."[88]

---

[88] Isaiah 53:7, as quoted in Acts 8:32

I had read many passages talking about the "servant". These did not seem always to refer to the same person, and sometimes clearly applied to the whole nation of Israel. One or two cases seemed probably to refer to Isaiah himself. It was all very puzzling, and I looked at it again before retiring to my bed that evening. My prayers that night were full of thankfulness for the window of comprehension newly opened by this precious scroll, but also of requests for help in my quest to understand who God's servant was. How could I guess that his answer would be provided so soon!

☙

Another early morning start and we were soon in the barren, desert areas of this road to Gaza. My reading continued, concentrating on the references to the "servant", as they had a strange fascination for me.

Our travel slowed until my driver was picking his way carefully through large potholes and areas of soft mud. Despite his care, I was still being tossed around in the chariot, and I stopped reading for a moment to look up. Obviously, there had been some rain in the recent past, and the road had been badly damaged. Walking along a ridge, a little distance above the road, I saw a man – obviously keeping out of the mud and slush on the road. I wondered idly what his business was, but quickly went back to my reading. I had come to the same passage that had puzzled me the night before. First it spoke of the servant prospering, being high and lifted up (which also reminded me of Isaiah's vision of God at the start of his prophecy, but I had no time to look back at that). After suggesting that there was something that would be hard to believe, the passage seemed to speak of the servant being oppressed and afflicted; led like a lamb to the slaughter. What could it mean? Of whom was it speaking? Was this Isaiah? I had no idea, but I couldn't give up trying to understand – and praying for help to do so.

And that was when the most amazing incident of my entire trip began. A voice, suddenly, at my elbow: "Do you understand what you are reading?" What a shock – although I laughed about that afterwards because it was the quickest answer to prayer that I had ever heard of in my life! The man I had seen walking beside the road was now right next to me. I doubted that he would be able to help me, but it was worth a try.

"How could I, unless someone guides me?" I responded. I was getting a little frustrated by the mysterious prophecies. I slid across to the other side of the chariot and motioned with my hand for him to sit next to me. He climbed in and sat down.

"I can see that you are reading from a scroll of the Hebrew Scriptures, but exactly which passage are you reading?"

"The part I really don't understand is this:

> 'Like a sheep he was led to the slaughter
> and like a lamb before its shearer is silent,
> so he opens not his mouth.
> In his humiliation justice was denied him.
> Who can describe his generation?
> For his life is taken away from the earth.'[89]

---

[89] Isaiah 53:7-8, as quoted in Acts 8:32-33

"About whom is Isaiah speaking?" I asked. "About himself or someone else?"

This was the start of a sublime lesson in understanding Bible prophecy. My advisor, who introduced himself as Philip, explained to me what this passage meant, and it fitted in perfectly with what I had been hearing in Jerusalem. Many in Jerusalem had been speaking about a teacher called Jesus, who had been crucified by the Romans at the insistence of the Jewish chief priests. In conversation, senior religious leaders had made it clear to me that this topic was off limits, but I had heard some detail from others.

Philip showed me clearly that the servant was Jesus of Nazareth, and he also explained many other passages from the Psalms, the law and the prophets. Some we could look at immediately in my new, treasured scroll of Isaiah. Philip knew the words of the passages he wanted, and I could find them quite quickly – one advantage of having already read the scroll several times.

The passages from the law and the Psalms I was familiar with, but it felt as if a light had been switched on – the meaning was now crystal clear. Most of the words of the Hebrew prophets I was not familiar with, prophets like Zechariah, Hosea, Daniel, Jonah, Amos and Micah. It is impossible to describe just how enlightening and exciting this was. I felt suddenly that I understood the world better, that the God I had worshipped as a loving and generous God was even better than I could ever have imagined.

All this time, my poor driver was taking extreme care, while the road conditions slowed our passage to a crawl. I have never felt so thankful for a bad section of road!

Philip explained the title "Christ" or "Messiah" as meaning "anointed" – like a king or a priest was – and showed me that Jesus was the Messiah prophesied. That he had died on a cross as prophesied, not because of any crimes he had committed, but rather because of his sinlessness, which had made the high priests jealous. Having become a little familiar with these men over the last month, I could easily see how true that could be.

Throughout this, I had my pen out, making as many notes as I could, though the roughness of the road made this awkward.

After teaching me about the prophecies regarding Jesus, Philip started to repeat some of Jesus' own teachings. These also were startling to me. As a non-Jew, they were immediately appealing, clearly referring to the lives of individuals, not the life of a nation of which I could never be a part. No nationwide feasts, no government, no army, no priesthood – just rules for life as separate people and families, under a single king-priest: Jesus. Philip had a small scroll with him of some of the teachings of Jesus, and we read over them together. It was a copy of a short history of the life of Jesus written by Matthew, one of Jesus' twelve special followers. Apparently, Matthew was still working on the history, but Philip had been lucky enough to get an early copy and had found it very useful in his preaching about Jesus.

What a day! From an early start, with a growing frustration at being unable to understand some passages in Isaiah, I had now come to understand more in one afternoon than in my entire life previously. But the best was still to come.

Philip told me about baptism. Jesus had commanded his followers to repent and be baptised into his name. Baptism was to be a symbol of dying and rising with Jesus: water being the tomb and rising from the water being like his resurrection, with a new life to follow. Philip explained that Jesus had been taken up into heaven after forty days of meeting with his followers, and that more than 500 people had seen him alive after his crucifixion and resurrection. He told of the miracles that some of the disciples of Jesus could do through the power of the Holy Spirit.

CR

Suddenly the driver let out a despairing groan. He slowed the chariot to a crawl and we saw that the road in front of us had been transformed into a wide sea of mud. Worse still, a sluggish stream of muddy water flowed across the road some distance ahead.

A small oasis[90]

---

[90] Sweet Publishing/FreeBibleimages.org:
http://freebibleimages.org/illustrations/philip-ethiopian/ Slide 9

Off to the right was a small oasis, with palm trees and green grass surrounding it. It had obviously been filled to overflowing by the recent rain. My heart leapt...what an opportunity!

"Look, here is water!" I cried. "What's stopping me from being baptised?"

Philip looked almost as excited as I felt, and he said, "If you believe with all your heart, you may."

"I do," I replied. "I believe that Jesus Christ is the Son of God!"

I leaned forward and said urgently to the driver, "Stop the chariot!" Almost before he had obeyed, I had climbed down into the mud and walked towards the edge of the small lake. Philip followed me a few moments later. The water was none too clean, but it didn't matter to me, and Philip was kind enough to climb down into the muddy water with me and baptise me in the name of Jesus.

We had clambered out of the water onto the bank of the pond, slipping and sliding, laughing with the joy of my newfound salvation, when Philip's voice suddenly stopped. I turned, and he was gone. Nothing was left except his footprints in the mud, slowly filling with a trickle of water.

As I look back on our discussion now, I can't see how we ever managed to cover so many different subjects in just a few hours, and yet so thoroughly. It was such an incredible time, so convincing, spiritually uplifting and enlightening. So utterly God-blessed.

Alone now, I walked back to my chariot, dripping with the water that had washed away my sins and given me such hope and joy.

CR

As I climbed into the chariot, my eyes fell upon my pen, lying next to a small scroll. It was Philip's precious copy of Matthew's good news about Jesus. On the outside of the scroll, Philip had written my name.

Twenty-Two

Praise Can Open Doors

For the true story, read Acts 16:16-40.

Silas watched as Paul cured the slave girl, never suspecting that such a simple act of kindness would cause so much trouble. Paul's frustration had been building over the last few days, so Silas was not surprised when he finally let out his annoyance and cured her. They were both familiar with the difficult decisions that had to be made when the power of God's Holy Spirit was available for immediate use. It was a big responsibility, and Silas was very willing to leave the decision to Paul. Paul was the leader anyway.

After being cured, the girl at first looked a little lost; as if she had just woken up. Her owners, waiting at the head of the street, took little notice at the time; they had become used to this daily performance of shouting after Paul and Silas, and found it quite valuable for attracting business to their fortune-telling stall.

Paul and Silas walked on together, out through the city gates to the place of prayer, which was their destination. The girl walked quietly back along the street with none of the extravagant hand waving, exaggerated head movements and other theatrics that had characterised her actions before Paul had healed her. Peace now reigned on the street as it had begun to reign in her mind.

The morning activities at the place of prayer began well, with several men and women already waiting eagerly for them to arrive and continue the teaching of the previous day. Silas greeted them warmly while Paul immediately singled out one of the men and picked up the threads of the last question asked the day before. The group settled down comfortably together around Paul at the edge of the river while he enthusiastically explained the revelation of Jesus in the prophecies of Isaiah in the Hebrew scriptures.

Silas made sure that everyone was comfortably within earshot and then sat at the edge of the group, watching their faces and interrupting occasionally to explain Paul's words a bit when any of the audience looked too lost. Silas enjoyed watching the light of understanding flare in someone's eyes as a niggling point of confusion found sudden clarity.

Paul was intense; a driven man. Silas enjoyed his company and found him an inspiring leader. But Silas contributed in a more relaxed style. He was not the leader of the small group of believers, but he didn't want to be either. A position of second in command suited him much better.

Discussion continued, calm and gentle mostly, but quite fiery at times; knowledge was shared; companionship developed; friendships built. During a lull in Paul's rapid-fire exposition, Silas took the opportunity to describe the healing of the young girl that morning. Someone suggested that they should pray for her, that she would be able to recognise God more clearly now that her mind was less tormented. Together, they knelt at the riverside, and Silas tried to express the thoughts and wishes of all in prayer to God.

It was Silas who first saw the group of men coming towards them. They were stopping from time to time, obviously asking questions, and people were answering and giving directions. Silas turned to watch them and thought he recognised two of them as the owners of the fortune-telling slave girl. He began to feel some concern, but still sat, waiting. Paul had his back to them and continued answering a tricky question until he was interrupted.

"That's them!" said one of the owners, excitedly.

"You're right," said the other, truculently, and he stopped and stood defiantly with his hands on his hips. "Now, see here," he began, "this trouble you've caused today. What are you going to do to fix it?"

By this time, Paul had turned around to face them. "What trouble do you mean?" he asked, puzzled.

"You and your religion," the truculent one responded. "You Jews aren't welcome here. You keep interfering and causing trouble. Our slave girl was just fine until you interfered. Now she's no good for anything."

"You mean she can't make you any money now that she's well?" answered Paul, a little sarcastically.

"Well, how can she?" responded the man. "She's lost all of that interesting character she had. Now she's just a boring, ordinary slave girl, like thousands of others. No imagination or fascinating ways. No opportunities for income now."

"What was she like when you bought her?" asked Silas. "Was she alright then or did she get like this later?"

"Don't you start suggesting that it's our fault she was like that," snarled the first owner.

"Well, aren't you glad she's normal now anyway?" asked Silas, gently.

"Normal? What's the use of normal? How does that help us? What use is she now?" shouted the other aggrieved owner, getting angrier with every exchange.

"Surely she can be more useful for God and for society now that she can think straight?" insisted Silas. It was clear that things were getting out of hand, but maybe some gentle answers could still settle things down.

"You can keep your God for yourself, instead of interfering here," yelled one, stepping towards Silas, while the other took several steps towards Paul. "You Jews go all around the world causing trouble, trying to get us Romans to do things that our laws won't allow. You've ruined our income and now you're going to pay for it!" he ranted as he grabbed Paul's cloak.

Their supporters joined in the attack on Paul and Silas and soon the two were being marched back up the hill and in through the city gates, having been struck many times by the men despite their lack of resistance. Silas was sporting a slightly swollen face that was obviously going to become a black eye.

"Let's take them to the magistrates, they'll know how to deal with criminals like these," said the truculent ringleader. The others agreed, and Paul and Silas were dragged along the main street by their assailants, with a man hanging on to each arm.

In the marketplace, the magistrates listened to the impassioned arguments of the slave girl's owners. These arguments made no mention of the slave girl, instead alleging solely that Paul and Silas had been promoting practices which were illegal for Romans to follow. The magistrates made no attempt to ascertain whether the claims were true or false, but instead ordered that Paul and Silas be beaten immediately. Silas was wearing a new-looking tunic and the chief magistrate personally tore it off him and threw it on the ground. The other magistrates ripped off the remainder of his clothes and pushed him towards one of the lictors before turning their attention to Paul. Cheers arose from the bloodthirsty crowd as the rods rose and fell rhythmically, with no-one questioning the justice of the punishment they were inflicting. Paul and Silas were foreigners, so they must obviously be causing trouble!

After many blows had been efficiently applied, the beating stopped, and the bloodthirsty crowd began to move on in the hope of other entertainment elsewhere.

The magistrates directed the lictors to dress the prisoners and take them to the prison. After a beating like that, having the clothes put on their backs just added to the throbbing agony. Arriving at the jail, the chief lictor gave the jailer very strict instructions about them. Thrown ignominiously into the inner prison, they were also locked into the stocks, just to make sure.

Paul and Silas singing in the stocks[91]

Taking the torch with him, the jailer closed the door and locked it, leaving Paul and Silas sitting in the impenetrable darkness.

Exhausted and struggling in a sea of pain, Silas tried to find a way to lie down and rest, but it simply wasn't possible. A back so badly bruised and torn could not be rested on the ground, and the stocks allowed limited movement, certainly not the twisting around that would have made it possible to lie on his side or front. Paul was smaller than Silas and had a little more slack around his ankles in the stocks, but even so, there was no chance of comfort. Forward or backward, sideways or twisting, there was no way to arrange the tortured body or limbs to permit genuine rest.

---

[91] Sweet Publishing/FreeBibleimages.org: http://freebibleimages.org/illustrations/paul-silas-prison/ Slide 6

The hours dragged, and the pain didn't seem to lessen. Talking helped, and at some stage Silas groaned, "If we can't sleep, let's sing. It'll cover the noise of the rats, too."

"Alright," said Paul, "but if we're going to sing, we have to make it good. Silence is better than songs of praise that sound like a dirge."

So they sang. Ancient Hebrew songs of an age-old faith; new Greek songs reflecting the joy of a new salvation revealed in Jesus. Above all, they sang with a joy of feeling that gave no hint of the suffering that never left them for a moment. Silas sang with a mellow bass while Paul's lighter tenor highlighted the happiness of the deliverance the songs recounted.

Their songs echoed through the cells of the prison, spreading a blanket of peace over the troubled souls who listened. The initial grumbles from other prisoners at the unlooked-for sound had long since turned to rapt attention, and as midnight approached, all the prisoners were listening in the darkness as if a spell had been cast over them. Even the jailer – sitting alone at his table in the small room which crouched, low-roofed, over the locked door of the prison – even he listened as he filled out the lengthy forms describing the latest prisoners and their crimes. For him, the songs were a distraction, taking his mind away from work that must be completed before he could retire to his bed. But they were also a niggling conscience to him. He listened to the words and tried to reason them away. He would never have admitted how much he knew of the truths behind the songs, but at times he wondered whether this message offered him the salvation he so desperately wanted. Salvation – the word had a wonderful ring to it, but how could he achieve it? Was this message, presented so beguilingly on the warm air of a clear night, the salvation he longed for? But work called and he did his best to shut out the words and voices of his two most important prisoners. Soon afterwards, he finished his most pressing work and took himself off to bed. Sleep claimed him.

Down deep in the prison, Silas was holding the last long note of a song of praise to God when everything changed. It came with a roar, and suddenly the earth was rolling and swaying. He would have jumped to his feet, but the stocks prevented that. All he could do was to steady himself by desperately holding the top bar of the stocks which held his feet firmly in place. Then, just as the roar of the earthquake reached its peak, the bar came loose in his hands. Not only that, but there were heavy bangs from all around, which later proved to be the doors of the prison cells opening. It was a terrifying moment for Silas, with the immediate expectation that the prison would collapse on top of him. He turned to look at where Paul must be, invisible in the darkness, and shouted, "Are you alright, Paul?"

"Yes," Paul answered, "have the stocks come undone for you?"

By that time, the noise level was dropping quickly and Silas could reply without any need to shout, "Yes, let's see if we can find out what has happened." Standing up carefully, he stepped around the stocks and edged carefully towards where he remembered the door would be. His hands were held out in front of him and he moved them from side to side as he tried to find the door. "I'm just trying to find the door," he said. His fingers found a rough stone wall and quickly followed it to the doorway. Though bolted and locked from the outside by the jailer after their evening meal, the door now stood open. He could hear terrified shouts from the other prisoners coming through the gap.

"Paul," said Silas, quietly, "the door is over here."

"Okay," said Paul, "it's always good to know where the jailers will come from when they open the door."

"Paul," said Silas, even more quietly, "the door is already open."

"Ah," he responded softly, "that makes it interesting. Shall we go out?"

"I suppose so. There's no light out there, though."

"That's alright," said Paul. "We only want to find out what's going on."

Paul stood up and felt his way to the door and Silas led the way out. By this time they could hear what the other prisoners were saying and realised that the "coincidental" opening of their door had been replicated all over the prison. Every door stood open and the terrified prisoners were congregating in the corridors as each found that the first step to freedom was theirs to take.

A varied company of people found themselves talking together that night in the stone corridors of that prison in the Roman colony of Philippi. Mostly petty criminals and debtors who could not satisfy their creditors, they were an unhappy bunch with little to look forward to in life. Some were all for breaking down the door into the jailer's room before melting away into the darkness to seek a better life in distant parts. Others saw an opportunity for retribution and suggested that the jailer should be first to suffer as they repaid society for its perceived mistreatment of them. Some more practical souls had decided to climb the stairs and check the door that led to the jailer's room, the door through which they had all entered the prison – the only door to freedom. As these intrepid explorers felt their way slowly through the complete darkness, the plans and hopes of each of the prisoners ebbed and flowed according to their natures. After what seemed like interminable ages, the word was quietly passed back, "The door is unlocked!"

Excitement spread like a fire through the men. Some rejoiced at the carelessness of the jailer in leaving open the doors, while others breathed the name of their special god or goddess in gratitude. Silas knew exactly what Paul's response would be, and within a few seconds he smiled to himself as he was proved right; Paul could not keep his peace.

"Men," Paul said, speaking just loudly enough that all could hear. "This is no chance carelessness on the part of our jailer, nor is it the work of a collection of gods, choosing to work together for the first time ever. This is the work of the God to whom Silas and I were singing praises. The God who has shown kindness and love to all of you in your terror during the earthquake. He gave you hope when you felt like rats in a trap. This is the one God, the creator God who gives life and hope to all and is father of all."

Paul and Silas tried to calm the excitable group with reminders that although they were in prison for many different reasons, escaping from prison would not make their case any better. It was a difficult task and they might not have been successful had not the jailer chosen that time to open the door.

CR

The jailer had woken when the roar of the earthquake announced the coming terror. Powerless himself, he waited until the earth stopped heaving and then urgently lit the small lamp over his desk and began to look around. He saw no obvious damage, but decided to call his assistants so that they could undertake a full inspection together. The assistants lived in a building next to the prison and it took some time to find them, outdoors in the roadway as they were, frightened by the earthquake. He gave them instructions to bring lights to the prison then returned to his office.

The room looked unchanged until he noticed the bolts of the door leading down into the prison. They were open. Both of them. Strange, he thought, how could that happen? He remembered bolting the door because one of the bolts had been harder than usual to line up with its target hole. Now it sat open at the far end of its travel.

Never mind, all of the prisoners were locked inside cells; the outer door was just a precaution. Even so, he would go in and look. He made sure he had his short sword with him and opened the door carefully.

CR

A feeble light shone through the doorway, the jailer a faint silhouette of despair to the disappointed prisoners as he peered into the utter blackness at the foot of the stairs. He faintly saw some of the prisoners moving; heard them climbing the stairs towards him. He jumped to a natural conclusion: the prisoners were free down there, and some must have already escaped. He pictured the shame of a trial, the charge of failing in his duty. Better to end it his own way, an honourable death with no questions.

The jailer took a step backwards. Paul saw him draw his sword and grasp it firmly with both hands and understood both his fears and his plans.

"Don't harm yourself," Paul shouted, "we are all here!"

The jailer fears the prisoners have escaped[92]

The sword wavered and the jailer stepped into the doorway again.

"It's true," confirmed Silas, "not a man has escaped."

"Bring a light," the jailer shouted to his assistants, waiting cautiously outside, and a brightly flaming torch was quickly brought.

---

[92] Sweet Publishing/FreeBibleimages.org:
http://freebibleimages.org/illustrations/paul-silas-prison/ Slide 8

CR

In the early morning light, Paul and Silas returned to the prison. The day before had been eventful enough, but this one was even more exciting. Instead of ending his life, the jailer had taken the opportunity to seek a new and better life. He had taken Paul and Silas to his home and did what he could for their painful wounds. All the while, they had been answering his question, asked as he had trembled with fear: "What must I do to be saved?"

Paul and Silas gave answers to the jailer and his family and all had felt compelled to respond by being baptised in the name of Jesus.

As they returned to the prison, Silas reflected on the irony of events in the last day. A gift of healing given to a tormented girl had led to beatings and imprisonment. A sacrifice of praise made while suffering in prison had led to life and hope.

Praise could open doors, and suffering could save lives.

Free Download

Paul in Snippets

An 81-page PDF novelette by Mark Morgan.

The life of Paul painted from the Acts of the Apostles.

Get your free copy of *Paul in Snippets* when you sign up for the Bible Tales mailing list. As well as the eBook, you will receive a weekly email newsletter with micro tales, informative articles and special offers.

Visit **http://www.BibleTales.online/free-pins**

9 781925 587203